"I have an ap____ ___ ____
Pierce went on. "We could
spend our honeymoon there."

For some seconds Holly couldn't believe he had said
what she thought he had said.

Reading her mind, Pierce added, "Yes, that was a
proposal of marriage. Not a very romantic one,
perhaps, but I can promise you a romantic
honeymoon...."

"I can't believe you're serious," Holly exclaimed. "Why
would you want to marry me, of all people?"

"You're the only one, of all people, I have ever wanted
to marry."

"But you're not in love with me...are you?"

"I don't think being in love is the best basis for
marriage. Liking makes better sense. I like you very
much, Holly."

Anne Weale was still at school when a women's magazine published some of her stories. At twenty-five she had her first novel accepted by Harlequin Mills & Boon. Now, with a grown-up son and still happily married to her first love, Anne divides her life between her winter home, a Spanish village ringed by mountains and vineyards, and a summer place in Guernsey, one of the many islands around the world she has used as backgrounds for her books.

Books by Anne Weale

A Marriage Has
Been Arranged
Anne Weale

Harlequin Books

TORONTO • NEW YORK • LONDON
AMSTERDAM • PARIS • SYDNEY • HAMBURG
STOCKHOLM • ATHENS • TOKYO • MILAN
MADRID • WARSAW • BUDAPEST • AUCKLAND

ISBN 0-373-03474-1

A MARRIAGE HAS BEEN ARRANGED

First North American Publication 1997.

FOREWORD

Anne Weale writes: As this is my seventieth romance, an important milestone in my writing life, you may like to know something about how I reached it.

The ambition to be a storyteller was always there, from my childhood. But there are many directions a budding writer may take, and luck plays a major part in any career.

My first, most important piece of luck was to marry a man who was about to go to the other side of the world. At the time I was a twenty-one-year-old newspaper reporter and had never been out of England. Our honeymoon in Paris was my first experience of abroad, although my husband had been to most of the countries around the Mediterranean while he was in the Royal Navy.

Today, young people backpack to the farthest corners of the globe. When I was young, opportunities to travel, except in the services, were extremely limited. When, a few months after our wedding, I flew to Singapore, and from there to the small airfield in north Malaya where my husband was waiting for me, it was a great adventure, arousing a wanderlust that has never subsided.

After two years in Malaya, we came back to England and I turned my experiences into a romance. The unusual and authentic background gave it a better-than-average chance of being accepted.

My second piece of luck was being advised to send it to Mills & Boon, then a small family firm but now, forty years on, as Harlequin Mills & Boon, part of a vast publishing empire reaching a worldwide readership. It's unlikely that, with any other publisher, I would have had my stories translated into twenty-six languages.

In creating exciting characters, it helps to be the wife and mother of men who do adventurous things. Many of my fictional heroes have been inspired by the real-life activities of my husband and son. Most of this book was written while they were planning the expedition undertaken by the hero of the story and his friend.

In an American book about successful women, I read, "The man who believes that he should share domestic chores equally with his working wife is as rare as a black swan."

To have written seventy romances and five longer novels—more than four and a half million words—is a satisfying achievement. But I couldn't have written all those books if I hadn't spent the past forty-five years under the wing of a black swan.

One of the most poignant lines in literature was written by Robert Louis Stevenson: "Many lovable people miss each other in the world, or meet under some unfavorable star." The young women in my romances meet their loves under a favorable star, as I did.

From this milestone of my seventieth romance, I've paused for a brief, grateful glance back at the happy past—one of its many rewards being letters from readers, some of whom write interesting comments on each new Anne Weale title to reach their library or bookshop.

Now it's time to look forward, to enjoy that wonderful moment of writing Chapter One at the top of a blank screen on my word processor before typing the opening lines of another story.

CHAPTER ONE

THE last place Holly would have expected to meet Pierce Sutherland again was at half past six on a dark, chilly autumn morning outside New Covent Garden Flower Market, long since moved from its original *My Fair Lady* location near the famous opera house to an ugly modern building on the south side of the Thames.

Holly, obsessively punctual and usually too early for everything, had been the first person to join the organiser at the rendezvous outside Gate Four.

Now about twenty people, including several shyly smiling Japanese ladies who didn't appear to speak English, were drinking hot coffee provided by the friendly young woman organiser with a clipboard and list of everyone who had booked for 'A Guided Tour of Covent Garden with a Champagne Breakfast and Flower Demonstration'.

A luxurious, chauffeur-driven car glided to a halt a few yards away. A tall man stepped out on the offside, surveying the group of coffee-drinking women with the same arrogant stare that Holly remembered from the last time she had seen him, five years ago.

What in the world was *he* doing? she wondered. Her heart gave an involuntary lurch in case he recognised her. Not that it was very likely. He hadn't changed, but she had. She was a different person from the nineteen-year-old who had deliberately tested his sense of humour and found him totally lacking in the all-important aspect of a man's character.

'Never lose your heart to anyone unless they have a good sense of humour,' her father had warned her, in one of their last discussions about life and love. 'Watch out you don't get involved with a pompous ass. There are a lot of them about.'

Professor Nicholson had smiled as he'd said it, but his warning had been a serious one. He himself, after losing his first wife when Holly was three, had made a bad error of judgement in marrying her stepmother, the female equivalent of a pompous ass.

He knew it. His daughter knew it. His colleagues and friends knew it. Only the second Mrs Nicholson was unaware of it. Their relationship was not unlike that of Mr and Mrs Bennet in *Pride and Prejudice*: an erudite man bound to a pea-brained woman whose younger daughters were as silly as she.

But Chiara, the eldest of Holly's stepsisters, although not a clever girl, was both beautiful and sweet-natured. Together from early childhood, she and Holly had grown as close as real sisters. Holly saw herself in the role of Elizabeth Bennet with Chiara as the lovely Jane Bennet.

So far their lives had not reached the happy conclusion of Jane Austen's famous novel. Holly had yet to meet anyone as compellingly attractive as Mr Darcy and Chiara was in a relationship unlikely to lead to permanent happiness. Their lives, so much freer and fuller than the stiflingly restricted lives of Jane Austen and her contemporaries, were still beset by the same basic problem: how to find Mr Right in a world full of Mr Wrongs.

Five years ago, Chiara had thought Pierce Sutherland was her Mr Right. Holly had always had reservations about him, and her fears had proved correct. Three months after taking Chiara to bed, Pierce had replaced her with another beautiful girl. The end of the affair had left Chiara with many generous mementoes of his transient passion for her, and it was an exaggeration to say that he left her heartbroken. Not long after their breakup she had been involved in another affair.

But that didn't alter the fact that Pierce had behaved like a rat, confirming Holly's instinctive distrust for him.

The other passenger in the stately Rolls-Royce was an elegant Japanese lady who seemed to be someone of importance, judging by the excited twittering among her compatriots. She waited for Pierce to come round the back of the car to join her.

When he did, the top of her sleekly coiffed hair was barely level with his chest and her pale, exquisite complexion and delicate features were a striking contrast to his tanned skin and rugged bone structure. Yet they did have something in common. She was dressed in a reversible cashmere shawl draped over a soft wool suit which undoubtedly had a top designer's label stitched inside it. Her leather boots and her bag were of the finest quality. She had style, and so did Pierce. Even Holly couldn't deny him that. Today he was wearing black trousers and a black cashmere turtle-neck sweater under a pale grey jacket that matched his cold light grey eyes, which were in striking contrast to his black hair and eyebrows.

By birth an American, by inclination an Anglophile, Pierce had come to England as a Rhodes scholar at Oxford University. He had never returned to his own country, preferring to have his main base in London and two or three *pieds-à-terre* in other parts of Europe.

Unlike Holly's father, who had spent his life on research projects of benefit to humanity, Pierce was a selfish man who used his brains for his own ends. When Chiara had met him, he had already been rich. By now he must be rolling. Whether he did a whit of good with his money, apart from giving lavish presents to his popsies, Holly was inclined to doubt.

Now, his hand under his companion's elbow, he steered her towards the organiser. While she exchanged gracious bows with her compatriots and the Englishwomen, he had a low-voiced conversation with the girl in charge of the tour.

Holly was too far away to hear what was said but, while his attention was focused on the organiser, she was able to study his face, looking for evidence that his sybaritic life-style was beginning to tell on him. Surprisingly, she could see none of the usual signs of high living. His jawline was still clear-cut, his waistline as lean and taut as it had been the first time she'd met him. He must be thirty-five now, but looked as fit and tough as men ten years his junior whose lives were extremely active, not spent, as his was, behind a desk doing deals. The expression 'fat cat' had been coined for men like Pierce Sutherland. Yet he didn't fit the image it conjured up. Physically, there was nothing soft, sleek or visibly decadent about him.

After he had dumped Chiara, Holly had forced herself to forget about him. It had been surprisingly difficult. He was one of those people of whom it could truly be said once seen, never forgotten. But she hadn't thought about him recently and the last thing she wanted was to renew their acquaintance. She was still eyeing him with disfavour when the demonstrator arrived.

'Good morning, ladies,' she said loudly, ignoring Pierce's presence. 'As there are thirty of you, we're going to split you into two groups. While I'm showing one group round, Lucinda will take the rest of you to the shops selling accessories. Then we'll change over.' She began to count heads.

To Holly's relief, the outcome of this exercise was that she was in Lucinda's group and Pierce and his companion were in Mrs Challoner's group.

Inside Gate Four, the market was revealed as a huge hangar-like space divided into blocks by a grid arrangement of wide aisles. Suspended from the centre of the roof was a big blue clock with a bell above it. Mrs Challoner's group went in one direction, Lucinda's in another.

Her circuit of the shops selling many kinds of baskets and vases, reels of plastic ribbon, florists' wire and Christmas garlands and decorations was over some time before Mrs Challoner had concluded her tour of the flower and plant stands.

While Lucinda's group were wandering about, waiting their turn to go with her, a woman in a red jacket said to Holly, 'I wonder who the tall guy is? Do you suppose he's a bodyguard? The Japanese person with him looks as if she might be Mrs Mitsubishi or Mrs Toyota…one of their multimillionaires' wives. Whoever she is, the guy with her speaks fluent Japanese.'

'How do you know that?' asked Holly.

'I passed them just now,' said Red Jacket, with a gesture at the aisle intersecting the one where they were standing. 'I heard him translating for her…with the other Japanese listening in. I'm surprised they come to a thing like this if they can't speak English.'

'Perhaps they can understand it better than they speak it,' said Holly. 'They may be married to businessmen and have time on their hands while their husbands are attending meetings.'

When it was time for the groups to change leaders, this took place without Holly being noticed by Pierce.

Considering that he was notorious for his roving eye, and that, apart from Lucinda, she was the only young woman in either group, she found it a tad deflating that he hadn't even given her a glance. But the parts of her which might have caught his eye—her legs and her figure—weren't shown to best advantage by the warm clothing they had been advised to wear. In navy blue trousers and a yellow foul-weather jacket over a bulky sweater over a long-sleeved T-shirt, she had no visible shape, and her face had never been her fortune. There was nothing really wrong with it. Her skin was clear, her eyes large, her good teeth the result of a healthy diet and good dentistry. But even when she was made-up and dressed to kill she wasn't a knockout like Chiara.

'Pleasant' and, possibly, 'nice' were the words she felt people would use if asked to describe her. She didn't merit the superlatives applied to her stepsister, nor did it bother her. Holly had never longed to be beautiful. She was comfortable with the way she was. Her mother hadn't been a beauty but her father had fallen in love the first time he'd seen her, and been desolated by her death. Someday, Holly hoped, someone would feel that way about her. Someone good, with decent moral values—not a womanising beast like Pierce.

The room where they were to have breakfast was up a staircase leading to the first-floor gallery.

It was an L-shaped room with a circular table in the angle of the L and several long tables filling the rest of the space. As soon as everyone was seated, staff began going round with bottles of champagne and jugs of chilled orange juice for those who wanted the wine in the form of Buck's Fizz or what two Americans present called 'mimosas'.

Holly preferred her champagne neat. As she had come

by taxi, having stayed overnight at Chiara's flat, to which she would return for lunch before catching a train back to Norfolk where she was living and working, she didn't have to restrict herself to one glass like those who had come here by car.

Pierce was seated with his back to her at a table which, apart from him, was exclusively Japanese. He was holding forth in that language and evidently telling a joke for suddenly there was an outburst of laughter, not the sound made by Europeans but a gentle tinkle of titters as all the dark eyes gleamed with merriment and ivory hands covered their owners' mouths.

After her first surprise that Pierce should speak their language, Holly realised it was probably not because he was drawn to Japan by its culture but because of its power as a trading nation. The making of money was his principal interest. Very soon, so she had heard, Japan would be in control of all the world's biggest and best electronics industries. No wonder he wanted the advantage of being fluent in that language.

As she ate croissants and crumpets and took a minor part in the conversation at her table, her gaze was repeatedly drawn to the broad shoulders and tanned quarter profile of the only male in the room, apart from a waiter serving coffee.

When most people had finished eating, Marisa Challoner rose to begin her demonstration.

'I suggest that those of you sitting with your backs to me should turn your chairs round rather than craning over your shoulders,' she began.

Holly had no need to move because from where she was sitting she had a good view of the demonstration table. But to her slight alarm she saw Pierce changing his position. From now on he would only have to turn his head a little

to the left to be looking directly at her. She could only
hope his role as an interpreter would keep his attention
fixed on Mrs Challoner.

As she opened a small exercise book and prepared to
make notes, Holly debated resting one elbow on the table
and shielding her face with her hand. Then she chided herself for being stupid. Of course he wouldn't recognise her.
They had met only once, at that deadly stuffy dinner party
when, according to her stepmother, she had behaved dis-
gracefully, proving herself to be both bad-mannered and
childish.

Actually, apart from Mrs Nicholson, Chiara and Pierce,
everyone had either roared with laughter or been convulsed
with giggles. But he hadn't seen the joke. She could still
remember the icy look in his eyes and the unamused set of
his mouth.

The demonstration held everyone mesmerised by the
clever way in which, with unpromising materials, Marisa
Challoner created an arrangement worthy of a luxurious
drawing room. As she worked, she chatted about her most
exciting commissions. The five-hundred-pound bouquet to
be sent to a film star. The recording star's lavish wedding
for which, out of a million-dollar budget, a hundred thousand dollars had been allocated for flowers. The summer
cruise in a millionaire's private yacht which she had been
asked to decorate with flowers worthy of the haute couture
clothes worn by the guests for dinner.

It was when, at the end of her talk, Mrs Challoner looked
round the room and asked, 'Any questions?' that Holly for-
got about keeping a low profile and was one of the people
to raise a hand.

Before she had time to reconsider this rash act, she had
caught Mrs Challoner's eye.

'Yes, what's your question?'

Stating it, Holly knew she was now engaging the attention of the one person in the room whose notice she had wanted to avoid. Increasingly aware of a pair of ice-chip grey eyes focused on her face, she scarcely heard a word of Mrs Challoner's answer to her query.

When, during the next question, she sneaked a quick glance at Pierce, he was still watching her. As their eyes met, he inclined his head, a clear signal that he had recognised her and would come over when the proceedings finished.

A succession of eager questions gave her ten minutes to brace herself for the encounter. She wondered what he would say. Perhaps he would ask about Chiara. As photographs of her stepsister were often in the gossip sections of the glossies and the tabloids, he could hardly fail to know that his affair with her had led on to other relationships of an equally ephemeral nature. In Holly's opinion he had set Chiara on the road to her present life of reckless pleasure-seeking with other people picking up the bills. Most of them older men. Some of them married.

Holly was repelled by her stepsister's way of life. It caused her almost as much pain as if Chiara were hooked on drugs. They had argued abut it endlessly, Chiara refusing to see why she shouldn't make the most of her one asset, her looks.

Around her, people were putting on coats and agreeing it had been a fascinating experience, well worth the cost.

'It's been a long time,' said Pierce, looming over her. 'How are you, Holly?'

She was astonished that he remembered her name, even if it was an unusual one. 'I'm well... And you?' she responded, with frigid politeness.

'Very well, thanks. Are you living in London now?'

'I came up specially for this. I'm based in Norfolk.'

'Are you married?'

She shook her head.

'Working?' he asked.

'I'm a garden designer.'

'It must be a satisfying job...providing you can get enough commissions to keep you going. Has the economic downturn been hard on you? Or do you work for a firm sufficiently well-established to survive the hard times?'

'I work for myself. I'm surviving. How about you? Still wheeling and dealing?' She couldn't disguise her contempt for a life spent manipulating the profits of other people's hard work.

'You could say that. Not quite in the same way as when Chiara and I were together. How is she? Still a playgirl, or has she settled down now?'

'It was you who made her a playgirl.' Holly hadn't meant to start a row with him here, but his casual enquiry riled her, reviving the impotent animosity she had felt towards him before.

'I wouldn't say that,' Pierce said equably. 'Chiara had several amorous adventures before I came on the scene. A girl with her looks was bound to attract a lot of men. She knew the score. You were the one with romantic illusions about life.'

There being no one close to them, she said in a low, angry voice, 'Considering we hardly spoke to each other, I consider that statement a bloody impertinence.'

It was rare for her to use swear words, but the bold way he had confronted her, as if expecting a welcome, made her furious. She longed to cut him down to size.

He said, 'Chiara often talked about you. She was worried that you would be hurt...that you weren't equipped to cope with people who didn't share your ideals. She felt losing your mother very young, and then your father, had made you vulnerable. I didn't agree. I thought you sounded tougher than you looked.'

'Streetwise enough to see through you,' she retorted. 'I knew you would ditch Chiara as soon as she began to bore you. I didn't like you then, Mr Sutherland, and I don't want to know you now. I'm amazed you have the gall to approach me. If you had a shred of conscience, you would have slunk out of here with your tail between your legs.'

Then, as she was about to add a frosty 'Excuse me' his Japanese friend appeared at his elbow. Speaking perfect English with hardly any accent, she said, 'I am ready to leave when you are, Pierce. Perhaps we can give a lift to your friend. They say it is raining outside now.'

When Pierce introduced them, politeness forced her to mask her annoyance with him while she spoke to Mrs Shintaro.

'Did you come here by car or taxi, Miss Nicholson?' the older woman enquired.

Holly was tempted to lie. But if it was raining heavily she didn't want to get soaked looking for a cruising taxi in an area where there might not be many, if any, for hire.

The previous afternoon she had been to the Bankside Gallery to see an exhibition of paintings of gardens. It, too, was south of the river, on the far side of Blackfriars Bridge. Afterwards, outside the gallery, an elderly lady walking with the aid of sticks had been almost in tears because of the dearth of taxis to take her back to the West End. Afraid of being mugged, she had begged Holly to stay with her. When, after a long wait, a taxi had finally appeared, she had insisted on giving Holly a lift in it. Now, in spite of her reluctance to prolong the encounter with Pierce, perhaps it made sense to accept a lift in Mrs Shintaro's limousine.

Five minutes later, sharing the back seat of the limousine with Mrs Shintaro while Pierce sat beside the driver, Holly was glad she had. The rain was bucketing down, and as they crossed Vauxhall Bridge she saw a pedestrian's umbrella blown inside out by the wind gusting down the river.

'It was kind of Pierce to come with me for, although I speak English well, with any technical subject there are always unfamiliar terms,' said Mrs Shintaro. 'He is a brilliant linguist and, as you may have noticed, was a great help to my compatriots whose English was not very good.'

'I thought it brave of them to come. What did they think of the demonstration?' Holly asked. 'Mrs Challoner's way of doing flowers is so different from ikebana.'

'You know about ikebana?' Mrs Shintaro looked surprised.

'I don't know much,' said Holly. 'Only what I read in a book by Shusui Komoda.'

Pierce turned to join the conversation. 'Holly tells me she's now a garden designer, Fujiko. The last time we met, five years ago, she was at college and I was dating her sister who is two years older.'

'You make it sound like a boy-and-girl romance,' Holly said coldly. 'It wasn't like that and you know it. You were thirty to her twenty-one, and you seduced her.'

She hadn't meant to revile him in front of Mrs Shintaro and the driver, but the angry accusation came out before she could stop it.

'I didn't seduce her,' Pierce said calmly. 'That was done in the back of a car by some upstanding young guy called Matt, or it may have been Mike. He enjoyed it. She didn't...and for a fortnight afterwards she went through hell, thinking she might be pregnant. With me she knew where she stood, she had a good time and she ran no risk of pregnancy.' Smiling slightly, he turned to the older woman. 'I hope these intimate details don't shock you, Fujiko, but this may be my only chance to correct Holly's misapprehensions.'

'I have lived in the West too long to be shocked or surprised by anything,' she said mildly. 'Is it true you treated your girlfriends unkindly when you were younger?'

'On the contrary, I was exceptionally nice to them. If you were to ask Chiara, I'm sure she'd tell you she had a very good time with me. We went to the Seychelles together. I gave her a Cappuchino sports car. We attended a lot of parties where she could show off the clothes charged to my account. Just before we called it a day, I bought her a ring she wanted.

'Chiara never gave me any presents,' he added drily. 'Except herself, of course. But apart from her face and her body she didn't have much to offer. Her general knowledge was limited. She had very few opinions. It was like making conversation with a rather dim fifteen-year-old. She may have improved since then, but five years ago I found her seriously boring.'

'That's vile of you,' Holly exploded. 'I've never heard a more disgusting example of blatant MCPiggery.' She turned to the woman beside her. 'You may not know the expression. MCP means male chauvinist pig and Pierce has to be the king of them. Would you please ask your driver to stop and let me get out? Another minute in this car and I'm liable to lose my temper.'

'No, no, it's raining too hard. You will be soaked to the skin,' said Mrs Shintaro. 'I have a better idea. We will all go to my apartment where you two can quarrel in private and get to the bottom of this matter. For I have to tell you, Miss Nicholson, your description of Pierce does not match *my* knowledge of him. My late husband, who was a good judge of character, thought very highly of Pierce. He has qualities not often found in Americans and Europeans.

Whatever happened with your sister was some time ago. He would not treat her badly now. Of that I am certain.'

Ignoring Pierce and forcing herself to speak quietly, Holly said, 'I'm sorry you've been involved in this clash between us. It was bad luck our paths crossed again. But I'm sure Pierce couldn't care less what I think of him. I don't like him and never shall. If your husband did and you do, then I hope he won't ever let you down.'

Diplomatically changing the subject, Mrs Shintaro said, 'I'm interested to hear you are a garden designer. England and Japan are both famous for their gardens, although, of course, they are very different in style. Where did you train for your profession?'

It was difficult to resist the warmth of her interest. She fixed her liquid dark eyes on Holly's face as if she were genuinely eager to have her question answered.

'I took a course at Denman's,' said Holly. 'It's a beautiful garden in Sussex where a well-known gardening writer has set up a school of garden design. After I'd got my diploma, I won a national competition for garden design and that led to two commissions. In the early stages, there's a lot of luck involved. But I had secretarial skills to fall back on if things went badly. I could always earn my living as a temp. That's someone who does office work on a temporary basis,' she explained.

'You sound very practical and sensible, but you must also be artistic. All the great gardeners are artists. Who has inspired you? Whose work do you most admire?' asked Mrs Shintaro.

This was a difficult question to answer without knowing how much, if anything, the Japanese woman knew of the history of English gardening and its most famous practitioners. But it sooned emerged that Fujiko Shintaro was far more knowledgeable than a great many English people and had visited many of the finest gardens in Europe.

Their conversation flowed with unexpected smoothness. Had it not been for Pierce's presence, Holly would have relaxed and enjoyed talking to one of the most interesting people she had ever encountered. She had always been drawn to the Japanese and sensed that in Mrs Shintaro she was privileged to meet someone special from whom, in other circumstances, she could have learnt much of value to her.

It seemed the liking was mutual, for, when the car drew up outside a canopied doorway in an elegant street not far from Grosvenor Square, Mrs Shintaro said, 'If you are not in a hurry, I would like you to see some paintings in my apartment. My driver will take Pierce home now and when we have finished talking he will take you wherever you wish to go.' To Pierce she added, 'We shall see each other at Catrina's opening on Friday. Thank you for coming with me this morning.'

He turned to her, smiling. 'It's always a pleasure to be with you, Fujiko.' His smile disappeared as he focused on Holly. 'Give my regards to Chiara when next you see her. I should be surprised if she shares your feelings about me. Try to be less judgemental, Holly. The first time we met, I liked you very much. Now you seem rather priggish…not an attractive characteristic.'

His sardonic tone made her livid. For the first time in her life, she experienced a powerful impulse to apply her fist to someone's face with all the force she could muster.

But Mrs Shintaro was already alighting from the car. Repressing her anger, Holly moved along the seat to be ready to step out after her.

When Pierce said, 'Goodbye,' she ignored him.

*   *   *

Fujiko Shintaro's penthouse apartment was the most luxurious place Holly had ever seen.

'Before I take you on a tour of my pictures, let's have some coffee, shall we?' her hostess suggested. 'But first you may like to wash your hands.'

She took Holly to a beautifully appointed cloakroom and left her to take off several layers of clothing made unnecessary by the central heating.

Among the many works of art which Holly saw during her time at the flat, one she particularly liked was a large bronze hand embellished with an elaborate bracelet or cuff and having a strange design engraved on the palm.

'Is this Japanese?' she asked, admiring it where it stood, the palm upturned, on a tabletop of thick glass.

'No, that was found in Nepal by my grandson,' said Mrs Shintaro, smiling. 'He has fallen in love with the mountains of the Himalaya. He noticed the hand in a Nepalese market. It was being used as a container for screws. He thought I would like it and bought it for me. It is one of my dearest possessions because he and I are very close. His mother was my youngest daughter. She married an American. They both were killed in a tragic accident when Ben was only eight years old. I did my best to comfort him and later, when I lost my husband, he did the same for me. It was through him that we met Pierce, who has a similar hand he also found in Nepal.'

When Holly made no comment, she went on, 'Pierce is also mad about mountains. With some men, they are a passion as powerful as love or religion.' She paused. 'If your sister doesn't feel any anger towards Pierce, why must you dislike him so strongly, Holly? Anger is a corrosive emotion. To hate someone for a long time is not good for the soul.'

'I haven't done that,' said Holly. 'Until today I had almost forgotten his existence. I *was* angry years ago, but you can't boil with rage indefinitely. The fact remains that even if he wasn't the first, it was Pierce who made Chiara realise her beauty was...well, to put it bluntly, a marketable commodity. Since her affair with him, her life has been a succession of liaisons with rich men. She doesn't love them. She uses them, the way Pierce used her. Wouldn't you feel as I do if he had done that to your daughter?'

Mrs Shintaro nodded. 'I'm sure I should feel very angry. How did your parents react?'

Holly explained that Chiara had only one parent—a mother not noted for her wisdom. When she had filled in their background, she said, 'Perhaps Pierce is a split personality who lives the way bigamists do, keeping different aspects of himself in separate compartments. He may not parade his girlfriends in front of his other friends.'

'It's possible, but I doubt it. He appears to have an unusually open nature. He often says things other people find shocking...as he did this morning. He was very frank about his relationship with your sister.'

'Egotistically frank!' said Holly. 'He sounded proud of himself...as if giving Chiara a car and taking her to the Seychelles made everything all right. The man has no morals at all. To him, women are commodities, not equals.'

'My views on equality are naturally different from yours,' said Mrs Shintaro. 'We are of different generations and cultures. All I can say is that to earn Pierce's respect a young woman would have to have exceptional qualities, because he—' She broke off as her Japanese manservant entered the room. He bowed before delivering a message.

Mrs Shintaro answered him in Japanese before turning back to Holly. 'My butler has reminded me that I have a luncheon engagement, which will be a great deal less enjoyable than lunching with you. However, I hope there'll be other opportunities. Do you come to London often?'

'I sometimes stay with my sister when she's at a loose end. She could come and stay with me, but she isn't keen on the country,' said Holly as they crossed the room.

'I should like to meet you again,' said her hostess. 'I'm interested in young people and especially in those, like yourself, who have chosen unusual careers. If you'll write your address in my visitors' book, we can keep in touch.'

On the train back to Norfolk, Holly wondered what Fujiko Shintaro would have said about Pierce had her butler not intervened.

She spent most of the journey thinking about him and about the old saying that a leopard never changed its spots. Anyway, just because their paths had crossed this morning, it didn't mean they would do so again. His world and hers were poles apart. Nor did she think it likely that Mrs Shintaro would keep in touch with her.

Remembering her mention of her grandson, Holly wondered what Ben was like. Often people with mixed blood were exceptionally good-looking, combining the most attractive features of both the races in their genetic make-up. Having American blood in him, he would probably be much taller than his mother and his grandparents, but perhaps retain the subtle ebony-ivory colouring that Holly had always found attractive, especially in babies—dear little solemn-faced bundles who, when sometimes she passed one in a pushchair, she felt an impulse to scoop up and cuddle.

Nowadays, merely tickling a stranger's baby under the chin was liable to be misinterpreted. But at least one could still make friendly overtures to other people's cats and dogs without being eyed with suspicion by their protective owners.

Holly had grown up with her father's black Labrador, Tom, but he, the most angelic dog one could ever have hoped to meet, had died of old age when she'd been ten. Now she had Parson, her cat, to lavish with love. Unlike many cats, who were affectionate only when they were hungry, Parson was always nice to her. Nobody had told him that cats were supposed to be aloof and capricious. He seemed to know she had rescued him from death by starvation when he was a kitten. Sometimes she wondered what would happen if and when she fell seriously in love. How would Parson react to sharing the bed he regarded as his and her territory with a third party?

So far neither of her two unsuccessful relationships had involved making love in her bed. What had happened—nothing ecstatic!—had taken place out of doors, in summer.

Perhaps, like the legendary Gertrude Jekyll, whose gardens and thoughts on gardening were still an inspiration to the garden gurus of today, she was destined to remain unmarried. In thirty years' time she too might be a guru, her name synonymous with some of the loveliest gardens in England.

In some ways it was a nice prospect. But it would have been even nicer if she could have been sure that in the years to come, on winter evenings, when she was browsing through nurserymen's catalogues and planning new plantings, there would be someone on the other side of the fire—someone who would look up from his book and say, 'Time for bed, darling, don't you think?' with a special warm glint in his eye to signal that it wasn't only sleep he was thinking about.

CHAPTER TWO

Two weeks later, on a bright, blowy morning in November when the leafless trees on the skyline gave the landscape the look of a Rowland Hilder watercolour, Holly stopped work at noon after an energetic morning's digging.

Having discarded her sweater a couple of hours earlier, she now slung it over her shoulders and was tying the sleeves in a loose knot when someone came through the arch in the old yew hedge and made her whole body quiver with consternation.

'Good morning,' said Pierce Sutherland, strolling towards her, taking in the evidence of her morning's endeavours. 'I was told I should find you here. Your cheeks are glowing like *Felicia* roses. Are you ready for lunch?'

'What are you doing here?' she demanded apprehensively.

'I felt like a drive in the country and I wanted to see you again so I twisted Fujiko's arm until she revealed where I'd find you.'

'I can't think why you should want to see me again when you know how much I dislike you...and always shall,' Holly said crossly.

'Always is a long time. You know what they say: Never say never. To predict that you'll always feel the way you do at this moment is a little rash, don't you think?'

'I can't see why it matters to you. You've already got

ninety-five percent of the female sex ready to dance to your tune. Why do you need me to succumb to your charm?'

'I'm attracted to you, Holly. I was the first time we met. But you were only nineteen, hardly out of the egg. I was thirty and involved with your stepsister. I thought what you did after dinner that night was the funniest thing I'd seen in years. I liked your sense of humour. You were the first girl I'd met who would dream up a gag like that.'

Taken aback, she was unable to hide it. All these years she had held it against him that he'd failed to see anything amusing in what she had done. Now he was telling her that, behind the mask of disapproval, he had been breaking up. Could she believe him?

'I'm told there's a very good pub a couple of miles from here. In the hope of persuading you to lunch with me, I booked a table before I left London. Will you lunch with me, Holly? Will you give me a chance to prove that, whatever I've done in the past, I'm not such a bad guy now?'

It was hard to refuse such a persuasive invitation, especially when it came from a man whose attractions could not be denied even by his worst enemy. This morning he was wearing pale blue jeans with a matching blue denim shirt under a darker blue canvas field coat with a yellow corduroy collar and corduroy linings turned back above his shirt cuffs.

In the sunlight, his thick black hair had the sheen of health and vitality. Like his brown skin and the clear whites of his eyes, it signalled a body in perfect physical condition.

'All right...but I still don't see why my good opinion matters to you.'

She picked up the worn canvas bumbag in which she kept her few necessities and slung it over her shoulder. Hopefully there would be a chance to comb her hair and put on lipstick when they arrived at the pub.

As they left the part of the garden where she had been digging to walk in the direction of the house being built for the couple she was working for, Pierce said, 'Tell me about this set-up. The house is new but the garden looks old.'

'The owner first noticed the place from the cockpit of his private aeroplane. Do you have a plane?'

'I do, but I didn't use it to get here this morning. Within easy reach of London I prefer to drive. The owner saw marks similar to crop marks, I presume?'

'Yes, the outlines of a large garden. But he found out the house that went with it had been demolished forty years ago. So he bought the site and had a new house designed which is smaller and more labour-saving than the original mansion. But the garden will be largely a re-creation of the one designed by Harold Peto at the beginning of the century. The yews were planted by him and a lot of other things are emerging from what seemed at first to be just tangled thickets.'

Surprising her with his grasp of the task involved, he said, 'Who's been responsible for the detective work? The owner or you?'

'Me mostly, and I've enjoyed it. I like digging up facts and following clues.'

'When will the job be finished?'

'The house is due for completion in the spring and the garden will be in place then, ready to hand over to the permanent gardener when they've appointed him or her.'

'What's next on your agenda?'

'Nothing definite. I've got various gardens I'm keeping an eye on. There's going to be a feature on one of them in the January issue of *House & Garden*. That may lead to some new commissions. How come you've heard of *Felicia* roses?'

'I noticed them at someone's house and asked what they were. I like to know what I'm looking at. The texture and colour of your cheeks reminded me of their petals. You were still in bud when we met before. Now, if you were a rose, you'd be ready to pick for the house or to be the focal flower in a painting by Fantin-Latour.' He slanted a quizzical smile at her. 'Yes, I've heard of him. Surprising, isn't it? You had me tagged as a total philistine, didn't you?'

'I wouldn't have thought nineteenth-century French flower painters would be of much interest to you,' she conceded.

'Everything's of interest to me. Life is like a vast warehouse, crammed with goodies from every corner of the globe and every century since the beginning of time. You have to rummage around and see what's on offer before you can make a choice of the things you want to select for your own treasure store. Some people never go beyond the section containing flashy ghetto-blasters, expensive cars, designer clothes and that sort of stuff. But I'm beginning to discover the things in the distant corners of the warehouse—things tucked away in cupboards or hidden under dust sheets, things you have to unearth. For example, Fantin-Latour.'

Holly was silent, stunned by the realisation that if this was how he looked at life he would have got on with her father. He, too, had seen the world as a place of wonder and delight, but had vacillated between anger and despair because most people's aspirations were so low, their horizons so narrow.

'When did you find your way into the gardening section of our metaphorical warehouse?' Pierce asked.

'My grandmother let me help in her garden. She gave me a plot of earth and some child-sized tools and a whole lot of seeds. It started from there.'

'Where do you live while you're working on this project?'

'I'm renting a summer holiday cottage. It doesn't have central heating but there's a closed stove which keeps the living room cosy. I've bought a trailer-load of logs and an electric blanket to keep me warm in bed.'

She spoke without thinking and instantly regretted it, feeling the glance he bent on her but determinedly ignoring it.

'Do you sleep alone all the time...even at weekends?'

'I never sleep alone. I share my bed with a very nice cat. He's been doctored to stop him prowling and yowling at night. It's a pity human tom-cats can't be neutered. It would save everyone a lot of trouble.'

Pierce laughed. 'No one would guess to look at you that you held such Draconian views. You look rather gentle, but clearly that's a false impression. Perhaps in an earlier life you were the high priestess of a matriarchal society in which most of the males were castrated at puberty apart from a few kept for breeding purposes. And even those wouldn't have been allowed to enjoy their masculinity for long.'

'I'm not a hater of men as a sex. I just object to those who have sex on the brain,' she retorted. 'I'm not flattered by being treated as a sex object. I dislike it intensely.'

'You could try wearing a burka, that long black garment that some Muslim women wear to avoid being admired by men. But I suppose it wouldn't be practical for the kind of garden designer who gets earth on her hands. Is that usual, a designer digging? I thought they spent more time using a slide rule than a spade.'

'I guess it depends on the designer. I find that work like digging helps me to sort out problems on the aesthetic side.'

'I find that too, but when I have a problem I go to my

club and swim. It's the same solution: repetitive physical activity makes the brain work better than it would if you sat staring into space.'

They had come to where the workmen had parked their cars. In the line-up of serviceable family cars, the instantly recognisable elegance of an old but well-kept Jaguar immediately drew the eye. She had expected him to have something ostentatiously and insanely expensive, but it seemed he didn't need the ego-boost of being envied by all the men for whom cars were a major status symbol. He had said as much earlier, but she hadn't quite believed him.

She was impressed by his manners. He opened the front passenger door for her and even pulled the seat belt out of its reel and handed it to her before closing the door. Most of the men she mixed with didn't do all that stuff. Some of them didn't even know it had once been standard behaviour. But she did because her father had had beautiful manners. She measured all men by him and found most of them wanting.

As he started the engine, Pierce said, 'Tell me about this very privileged cat of yours. I have a cat myself...a Maine Coon, if you know what that is. But we don't sleep together. She has a basket in the kitchen.'

'Maine Coons are large, with fluffy breeches, aren't they?'

'That's right. Breeches and ruffs and big personalities. My father's eldest sister was a leading light in the International Society for the Preservation of the Maine Coon. She was a strong-minded lady who didn't approve of Britain's archaic quarantine regulations. When she came on a visit, she smuggled Louisa, then a kitten, through Customs. Within five minutes of her arrival at my place, the household had expanded to include an illegal immigrant. Does that shock you?'

'It surprises me. Being, as you pointed out, very priggish, I wouldn't ever deliberately break the law.'

'Maybe not, but would you report someone who had?' he asked. 'Would you turn in your favourite aunt?'

'No, I wouldn't,' she conceded. 'And if the cat had had all the necessary shots I don't suppose there was much danger of it bringing in any diseases, certainly not rabies. One of my grandmothers who was a great traveller thought the British were totally paranoid about rabies.'

'The British are either some of the world's greatest adventurers or they're extremely insular and can't get their minds round the idea that there are other ways of life that might be better than theirs. But, having said that, I've chosen to live here in preference to where I was born and all the other places I could have settled. Getting back to cats…what breed is yours?'

'A common tabby, but he does have nice markings and a little white clerical collar, which is why he's called Parson. Sometimes he comes to work with me, but today he had gone through the cat flap before I got up. Luckily the people who own the cottage also have a cat, so Parson can come and go as he chooses. The downside of that is that often, when I get home, he's left something dead on the floor. Who looks after your cat when you're away?'

'I have a man and a daily. Hooper doesn't live in but he's around long enough for Louisa not to get lonely.' He took his eyes off the road for a moment to glance at her. 'Who would have thought, after the spat we had last time, that we'd be comparing cat notes in this companionable way? I suppose you realise that, if you had flared up at me in front of most Japanese, they would have been profoundly shocked. They go to extreme lengths to avoid confrontation. Politeness is deeply engrained in their character. They never have altercations or behave aggressively in public. To be impolite causes huge loss of face.'

'Mrs Shintaro seemed to take it in her stride. Afterwards she was very nice to me.'

'She's extremely broad-minded. Her whole married life has been spent adapting to other cultures and smoothing over situations which would never have arisen in her own country. When she was in her twenties, she must have been every man's dream of the perfect woman...beautiful, intelligent, loving and totally supportive.'

'Totally submissive is what you really mean, I suppose. But not *all* men want a woman to be a doormat. My mother was making her name as a radio producer. My father insisted on her keeping up her career. If she hadn't died, he would have gone on encouraging her to make the most of her gifts. He would have despised your attitude to women.'

'Perhaps his own was different before he met your mother,' said Pierce. 'My attitude to women depends on their attitude to themselves. If all they want is a good time, I'm happy to oblige them. You accuse me of leading Chiara down the primrose path, but I couldn't steer you in that direction, could I?'

'You wouldn't have succeeded with Chiara if she'd had a sensible mother,' Holly said shortly. 'My stepmother was fool enough to think you might marry Chiara. Instead of discouraging the relationship with you, she egged her on. I knew it would end in tears. That was obvious from the beginning.'

'But it didn't end in tears,' he said equably. 'Chiara wasn't heartbroken. She was never in love with me. You credited her with the feelings you would have experienced if a man you were involved with had called an end to the affair. At nineteen, you would only have done what your stepsister did if you had been in love...or imagined you were.'

Reluctant as she was to agree with him, inwardly Holly had to admit there was a good deal of force in his argument. Chiara had been upset, but it had been mainly wounded pride rather than real heartache which had been the cause of her tears.

'That doesn't alter the fact that you gave her a taste for high life and luxuries she couldn't afford except by...by selling herself to other men like you. You got her hooked on rich living in exactly the same way that other girls get hooked on drugs. And if you'd done that to her, I would have made you pay for it if...if I'd had to kill you myself,' Holly said quietly.

'Got hold of a gun and shot me?' He gave a soft laugh. 'Yes, I believe you would. But the fact is that Chiara had nothing more damaging than champagne while she was under my aegis. I smoked some pot in my teens but I drew the line at the rest of it. I don't need that kind of high. I've always found wine and women adequate stimulants. How about you? How do you get your kicks?'

'From my work mainly. But it's more a case of quiet satisfaction than kicks. Gardening might seem dull to some people, but in fact it's very fulfilling. There's always something to look forward to. I can't wait to see how this garden I'm working on now looks in two, three and four years' time. I suppose it's the same sort of gratification that people get from watching their children grow up.'

'It sounds a little tame for someone of your age. Don't you want excitement...adventure...nights of passion... mornings when someone rings up and persuades you to do something crazy?'

'I think you're taking the mickey. You can't charm me, so you mock me. There's something about women like me—women who aren't flattered by your attention—that irritates your ego.'

'Perhaps. But who knows? Like the grain of sand the oyster deals with by creating a pearl, our mutual irritation may eventually be transformed into an enjoyable friendship. Are you prepared to give it a try?'

'Not really,' Holly said coolly. 'I don't believe you're capable of friendship with a woman, any more than a leopard can be friends with a gazelle.'

Pierce made no comment on this, perhaps because they had reached the junction with a busy main road where he needed to give more attention to the traffic. Even after they had joined the stream of vehicles and were heading in the direction of the nearest market town, he didn't pick up her barb and toss it expertly back at her.

She wondered what he was thinking. Perhaps she had made a mistake in not accepting the proffered olive branch with outward grace and inward scepticism.

The pub which was their destination was two or three miles outside town, a little way off the main road. A large car park was an indication of its popularity but perhaps its main trade was at weekends, for today there were not many cars there.

The interior was 'ye olde worlde' but not off-puttingly kitsch.

'If you want to go and tidy up, the Ladies' is over there,' said Pierce, spotting the discreet sign before she did. 'What would you like to drink before lunch?'

Holly felt that his manner had suddenly changed to the avuncular attitude of a worldly man finding himself in charge of an exceptionally gauche teenager, like a long-suffering godfather taking an awkward sixth-former out to lunch in the absence of her parents.

She said, 'A vodka and tonic with ice but no lemon, please,' and headed in the direction of the loos.

There she discovered she didn't have a lipstick with her, only some colourless salve and a tube of cream, protections against chapped lips and hands. There wasn't much she could do to boost her self-confidence other than release her hair from the band tying it back at her nape. Swinging in a loose bob just above shoulder-level, it made her look slightly more sophisticated. But she would have given a lot to have some eye make-up, scent and a pair of earrings with her. Not because she wanted to look more attractive, but simply as boosts to morale.

Why did I let myself in for this? she asked her reflection in the mirror. Why didn't I say no?

With a thrust of annoyance she faced the vexatious answer to both those questions. In spite of what he had done to Chiara, in spite of her own strong dislike of him, she had come because Pierce intrigued her. She was drawn to him in spite of herself. Moths didn't know they would burn their wings by being lured by the light inside a lampshade. She *knew* Pierce was dangerous, and yet she couldn't resist this closer contact with him.

Chiara had been attracted by his wealth and his lavish lifestyle as much as by his looks and his powerful sex appeal. But Holly was drawn by the man behind the public mask. She wanted to know what made him tick and if, behind his appearance of total self-confidence, there were hidden weaknesses, parts of him which could be hurt.

Not normally cruel and revengeful, she found herself wanting to wound him, to exert the same sort of power he exerted on the women he made his playthings. She knew it was completely mad, but she wanted to have Pierce Sutherland in *her* power and make him know what it felt like to be treated the way he had treated Chiara. At the same time she knew she had none of the weapons she needed to achieve that objective: not beauty, not a brain to match his, not irresistible sex appeal…none of the things she needed to be able to play him at his own game.

Her only resource in dealing with him, the one thing which set her apart from all the other women he had known was her resistance to him. And how long would that be a safeguard if he decided to undermine it? She would be like the commander of a city under siege. She would have only two options, one of them to surrender.

Pierce was not at the bar when she rejoined him. He was sitting at a corner table, glancing at a copy of *The Times* which he had taken from a selection of newspapers and magazines on a table in the centre of the room. When he sensed her approaching, he tossed it aside and stood up, taking in her loose hair.

'I've already made my choice,' he said, indicating a menu lying on the table next to her drink.

After sating herself, Holly picked up the glass. She didn't say 'cheers' or anything similarly friendly before she took her first sip.

'I've a casserole ready for my supper so I won't have much lunch. I'm used to a sandwich and an apple at this time of day.'

'Do you like cooking?' he asked.

'I like eating. Where I'm living at the moment, it's cook or go without. The nearest take-away place is six miles away. Anyway, I'm not into junk food.'

'I can see that. You glow with health. I should think your breath is like sea air, even first thing in the morning.' As he said it, he smiled into her eyes.

The effect on Holly was catastrophic. Immediately, she had a vision of lying in a half-acre bed, under the lightest and most luxurious swan's-down duvet, with Pierce stretched out close behind her, propped on one elbow, both of them naked. And what she saw in her mind's eye caused such a strong reaction that she gave an audible gasp as sensations she wasn't prepared for shot through her insides like an electric charge.

To make matters worse she was almost certain he knew what was happening to her, had set out to have this effect and was amused and pleased at having achieved it.

'It's not difficult to stay fit when you're leading a natural life,' she said, trying to sound composed. 'If I worked in a city office, I would never feel well. I don't know how people survive that sort of environment, especially offices with no natural ventilation.'

'I agree.' Pierce picked up his glass and drank some lager. 'Given no other options, I would rather sweep leaves in the park than be a commodities broker. The lives those guys lead is inhuman. At the end of a twelve-hour day, all they're fit for is propping up a bar or snorting cocaine. And for what? Only money. No job satisfaction. No security. No esteem worth mentioning.'

'"Only money" is easy to say when you have plenty of it,' said Holly. 'I can't see you as a park sweeper; I really can't.'

'Neither can I,' he said, smiling. 'But luckily I was born with more than two options…almost unlimited options. All you need in this world is some brains and a lot of ambition and you can't go wrong. Whatever you want you can have, but you have to work for it. Look at you. You wanted to be a garden designer and you are. But I doubt if what you've achieved fell into your lap. You had to strive for it.'

'I haven't achieved much so far. I'm only at the beginning. But I think it's the kind of career which will mesh with the other things I want.'

'Which are?'

She gave him a level look. 'A husband and children. That old-fashioned thing called marriage which people like you despise.'

'Where did you get that idea? Because I didn't marry Chiara, it doesn't mean I don't want a wife when the right woman comes along.'

'And will you be faithful to her?' she asked. 'Or will you continue to have affairs on the side?'

He didn't reply immediately but gave her a long, thoughtful look which she found quite hard to hold.

'On the basis of very little evidence, you've jumped to a lot of conclusions which are about as accurate as the stories in the tabloid press,' he said. 'Tell me, are you exactly the same as you were five years ago?'

'Of course not, but five years ago I was still in my teens.'

'Yes, I remember you well,' he said, smiling faintly. 'You were wearing a dress that didn't suit you and your hair was badly cut, but even so you had something about you...the promise of how you are now.'

The caressing tone of his voice and the look in his eyes, which were not as cold as she had thought—or, at least, not when he chose to soften the expression in them—made Holly lower her gaze in the hope of masking her response.

Did he really remember her as clearly as he made out?

'The whole evening was an exercise in over-the-top pretentiousness,' he went on reminiscently. 'If there were a prize for bad taste, your stepmother would certainly be on the short list.'

'And you would be on the short list of guests who have no compunction about running down their hostess,' Holly said frostily.

'Oh, come on, Holly; I'm only speaking the truth. It was

making you cringe. I watched you. You wanted to sink through the floor.'

She couldn't deny it. She *had* cringed. But her father never had. Unlike Mr Bennet in *Pride and Prejudice*, Professor Nicholson had never by the flicker of an eyelid revealed the embarrassment his second wife's affected, snobbish behaviour had caused him. Only sometimes, alone with his daughter, had he permitted himself some wry comment which he knew he could trust her not to repeat to anyone. But, of course, by the time of the party under discussion, he had already died of a massive heart attack.

'I was having a bet with myself,' Pierce went on, 'that when all those piddling courses of second-rate food finally came to an end Mrs Nicholson would rise to her feet and sweep you all off to do whatever women do when they leave the men to drink port and "put the world to rights".'

The accuracy of his memory and the exactness with which he mimicked the arch inflection of her stepmother's voice when she'd made this remark made Holly smile in spite of herself.

'You are very unkind.'

He shrugged. 'I was massively bored by it all. You can't expect me to be kind about someone who put me through several hours of acute boredom. I was tempted to get up and walk out. Life is too short to sit through that sort of nonsense. It was only when we joined you in the drawing room that the whole thing was made worthwhile.'

Suddenly his face was alight with warmth and humour, his grin revealing the fine teeth she had only glimpsed while he'd talked.

'You were sitting by yourself on an uncomfortable chair, looking as if butter wouldn't melt in your mouth. And then, when the coffee had been passed round and the woman with the double-barrelled surname was holding forth in that falsely plummy accent, you suddenly crossed your legs and lifted your long skirt a little…revealing those huge hairy feet with claw-like toenails.'

He gave a deep bay of laughter, clapping his hand against the hard length of his thigh. 'I should think they could hear her shriek at the other end of the street. For a minute she thought those appalling great feet were real. Her eyes were on stalks. It's a wonder she didn't have hysterics.'

Remembering the expression on the face of the woman he was talking about, Holly began to smile and then to dissolve into laughter.

'But you weren't amused then,' she reminded him. 'You couldn't have looked more po-faced.'

'I was clenching my back teeth so hard, it's a wonder they didn't fuse. Inside I was breaking up. When I laughed about it later, Chiara was very annoyed with me. She didn't share your sense of humour. In fact I don't ever remember her belly-laughing at anything. The best she'd manage was a breathy little giggle. Now don't flare up and bite my head off. If we can't speak frankly to each other, we're never going to get anywhere. The bedrock of friendship is truth.'

'If that involves running down my sister, we're never going to be friends,' Holly informed him.

'I'm not running her down. I'm being honest. She's a beautiful girl but she has no sense of humour. Never in a million years would she have worn those feet in those circumstances. Where did you get them, anyway?'

'They were a present I'd bought for my best friend's younger brother's birthday. I'd always wanted a brother and Dan was the next best thing. When the others went up to my stepmother's bedroom, I went to mine, where the feet were waiting to be wrapped up. The reason I put them on was to test whether *you* had a sense of humour. I didn't think you were going to ask Chiara to marry you, but in case you did I wanted to run through the checks my father advised me to make on anyone I thought I was in love with.'

'And what were they?' Pierce enquired.

'The first was a good sense of humour. The others...I don't want to discuss.'

'Which means, I suppose, that they have to do with sex...a subject you aren't comfortable with...or, at least, not with me...not yet,' Pierce remarked drily.

His shrewdness was disconcerting. He made her feel he could see inside her head and read her thoughts, like someone illicitly accessing the files stored on another person's computer.

It was a relief when he said it was time they ate, if she had decided what she wanted.

Holly had half expected that his lunch would be the T-bone steak with French fries and grilled tomatoes and mushrooms. But when one of the barmaids had come to take their orders and Pierce had told her that his guest would have the cottage cheese salad with pineapple, his own order turned out to be stuffed peppers with a baked potato and a side salad.

To drink, he ordered spring water, asking Holly if she preferred it still or sparkling.

'Still, please.'

When the waitress had left them, he said, 'If I weren't driving, we could share a bottle of wine. But if you're working this afternoon you probably don't want to drink much either. By the way, I bring a message from Fujiko. If I succeed in healing the breach between us, she would like me to bring you to a party she's giving on the twenty-fourth. Her parties are always first-rate. I know you'd enjoy it. Will you let me be your escort?'

'Do I need an escort? Wouldn't I be acceptable on my own?'

'Of course, but rather than putting you to the trouble and expense of going to London by train Fujiko felt it would be easier if I fetched you in my chopper. The invitation includes a bed for the night...a bed in Fujiko's apartment. I can imagine your reaction if I offered you one at my place. Although if I did you would have nothing to fear,' he added quizzically. 'I never make passes unless I'm sure they'll be welcome.'

Holly ignored this sally. Did she want to go to a party under Pierce's aegis? What did her wardrobe include that would do for a smart London party which might be black tie? Nothing. Not even a little black dress, because she had never had that sort of social life.

'The reason she's giving the party is because her grand-son's coming over,' Pierce went on. 'Did she tell you about Ben? He's the apple of her eye, and deservedly so. He's a sweet guy. You'll like him. He's the antithesis of me,' he added drily. 'Kind, gentle, deeply chivalrous towards women. Ben is a combination of all that's good in two very different cultures. People like him are our best hope for the future. So...will you come?'

Holly took a deep breath, knowing instinctively that she could be about to make the worst mistake of her life.

'All right...yes...yes, I will.'

CHAPTER THREE

THE day before Mrs Shintaro's party, Holly went to London by train, intending to spend the next two nights with Chiara.

Two days after lunching with Pierce, she had telephoned him to say it wouldn't be necessary for him to fetch her in his helicopter. She had made other arrangements.

He accepted this decision without argument. Nor did he quibble when she added that she would also get to the party under her own steam and meet him there.

Perhaps he suspected she might be staying with her stepsister and preferred to avoid an encounter with his ex-girlfriend.

Chiara, when she opened the door of her Chelsea flat, was sporting a golden tan acquired on a recent visit to southern Spain where Eric, her current 'close friend', kept a yacht berthed at Sotogrande, a glitzy resort at the Gibraltar end of the Costa del Sol, or the Costa del Golf as it was sometimes known.

'*Darling*...lovely to see you.' She embraced Holly warmly. 'You look a bit peaky. Are you all right?'

'Couldn't be better,' said Holly. 'Just not as suntanned as you are. How was Spain?'

'Oh...not bad,' said Chiara, shrugging. 'I got a bit bored with the wall-to-wall wrinklies. The average age on the Costa has to be seventy at least. You hardly ever see a woman who isn't on her fifth or sixth face-lift...apart from a scattering of bimbos.'

It didn't seem to occur to her that many people would regard Chiara herself as a bimbo, Holly thought, with a pang.

Since her stepsister had been with Eric, she had taken to having her hair done an even lighter shade of blonde and to wearing increasingly *outré* clothes. Obviously Eric liked her to attract attention, but it wasn't the kind of notice which would have pleased Pierce when she had been with him. Under his aegis, Chiara had worn clothes by Armani and Calvin Klein, clothes in subtle good taste which Holly had had to admire even if she hadn't approved of Pierce paying for them.

But now Chiara was buying creations by the wilder, most way-out designers, and although they cost a lot of money somehow they made her look cheap.

'I didn't expect you to come up again so soon after using the flat while I was away,' she remarked on the way to the living room. 'What brings you here this time? More research work?'

'I want to do some Christmas shopping…and I need to find something to wear for a party tomorrow night.'

'A party in London? How come?'

While Chiara made coffee, Holly explained about meeting Mrs Shintaro at New Covent Garden and being given a lift because it was raining heavily. For the time being she left Pierce out of it.

'How exciting!' Chiara's pansy-dark eyes glistened with interest. Parties, and planning what to wear to them, were the breath of life to her. 'But you don't need to buy anything, silly. Have a look through what I've got. There's bound to be something you'll like.'

Although it was seldom apparent to other people, because they presented themselves in totally different ways, Chiara and Holly had almost identical vital statistics.

Later, after coffee and when Holly had unpacked in the spare bedroom, Chiara took her to her own bedroom where a long bank of built-in closets housed her extensive wardrobe.

One of Chiara's most likeable characteristics was her generosity. She had always been happy to share her things with her sisters and stepsister.

Now, for Holly's delectation, she showed all her most recent buys, including a selection of what she called 'LBDs', meaning little black dresses, but not of the discreet, undating standby variety. The ones she had picked out all made strong, sexy statements which Holly lacked the panache to carry off.

For a moment, as Chiara held against herself a barely-there sheath of clingy crushed velvet which would mould to every curve of her body in explicit detail, Holly wondered how Pierce would react if she went to the party showing maximum cleavage and leg.

But it wasn't her style. Never had been and never would be. She didn't want men's eyes crawling all over her as they mentally stripped off the little she was wearing. She wanted to look alluring, but not to flaunt her sexuality.

The telephone rang and Chiara answered it. 'It's Eric. I'll talk to him in the living room. Have a look through. Try things on,' she said, indicating the other cupboards. 'Hang on a minute, sweetie. I'll be right with you. I've got Holly here. She's just arrived. We're going to spend the afternoon shopping...unless you have other plans for me,' she added, with a meaningful giggle.

Holly had never met Eric. She had only seen photographs of him posing on board his yacht in a peaked cap. He was in his late forties, had two divorces behind him, and Chiara said vaguely that his wealth came from pharmaceuticals. He looked to Holly as if he might be involved in something shady. Of all Chiara's men-friends, from what little she knew of him, she liked him the least and hated the thought of his picking up the bills which her sister had no means of paying herself, except by selling some of the jewels she had acquired.

Crushed tightly together in the other cupboards were garments which sooner or later would be given to a charity shop to make room for new things. Had they belonged to Holly, she would have taken them to a dress agency in order to recoup a little of what they had cost. But thrift was a concept beyond Chiara's grasp.

As her gaze coasted over the rainbow of vivid colours, looking for something more subtle, Holly's eye was caught by a sky-blue shoelace peeping out from between something made of yellow satin and its black lace neighbour. Investigating, she found that the shoelace with its matching metal tag was stitched to the sleeve of a lime-green jacket. Extracting it from the crush, she found there were other laces in other colours, stitched on like stripes with their ends left free. The colours were those found in a box of fondants: pink, lemon-yellow, lilac. The effect was charming.

Holly tried the jacket on. It wasn't her usual style, but it suited her. The statement it made was spring-like and carefree. It spoke of April in Paris, bunches of bright balloons, ice creams in many flavours. When she looked, the label said Moschino.

'Oh, heavens, that's ages old. I saw it on a display model when I was on the escalator at Harvey Nicks and I couldn't resist it,' said Chiara, returning. 'It's fun, but somehow not me. I've hardly worn it. It's lovely on you, though.'

'Did Pierce buy you this?' asked Holly.

'God, no! It's not *that* old,' Chiara said, amused. 'What ever made you think of him? Pierce was a *long* time ago.

All the stuff I wore when I knew him would look really draggy by now.'

'I ran into Pierce,' said Holly. 'He was at New Covent Garden with Mrs Shintaro. He's a friend of her grandson.'

'Did he recognize you?'

'Surprisingly, yes, he did.'

'He always had a fantastic memory. I could never get away with fibbing to him. He'd catch me out straight away.'

'Why did you need to fib to him?'

'Oh, I don't know…one just does,' Chiara said airily. 'Men are such tricky creatures. You have to learn to manage them. I didn't know that then and I handled him awfully badly. It was always he who called the shots.'

'Doesn't Eric?'

'Definitely not! I've got him eating out of the palm of my hand. The fact is, darling, that the entire male sex is so hooked on sex that when they're in need of a fix you can make them do anything you want. For women who understand that, anything is possible.'

Holly frowned. 'It sounds horrible…like pushing drugs.'

'I suppose it is in a way, except that it doesn't do them any harm or kill them. Well, it might if they were quite old and they overdid it, I suppose. But normally it just puts them in a good mood—the kind of mood when they'll give you the moon if you ask for it. I sometimes think I could write a best-seller—*How to Manage Men*. But really it's so dead simple that it wouldn't cover more than a couple of pages.'

On impulse, Holly said, 'Do you really enjoy having sex with Eric?'

Chiara gave a peal of laughter. 'No, but he does, and that's what counts.'

Holly said nothing. Her own view of sex had been

formed by her father who, long before she had started men-
struating, had given her a book which explained the work-
ings of her body and the reproductive process. Then, later,
at some appropriate moment, he had mentioned that physical love was one of life's most glorious experiences and,
for that reason, not to be undertaken casually, like lesser
pleasures.

'Any fool can jump into bed and they do...in droves,'
he had told her. 'If you can, hang on a bit, Holly. Wait till
you're seriously in love, because it makes all the difference.'

But of course she hadn't listened to him. Curiosity and
attraction had been the reasons for her first experience, and
loneliness and attraction had propelled her into the second.

Chiara said, 'Let's have a look for a skirt you could wear
with that jacket. Not black—that would be too heavy for
it. Something to pick up the colour of one of those sneaker-
laces.'

As Chiara had a date with Eric that evening—they were
going dining and dancing with another couple—Holly took
herself to the theatre. The others were still on the town
when she returned.

The last time she had been to the theatre in London, she
had gone to sleep thinking about the play. Tonight it was
Pierce who filled her thoughts. Reluctant as she was to
admit it, she knew she was looking forward to seeing him
tomorrow night. On her way to the theatre she had wondered if he might be there, his height and his thick dark
hair making him easy to spot even in a crowded auditorium.
But although she had scanned the front stalls and the boxes
from her seat in the dress circle, he hadn't seemed to be
there. She had felt absurdly relieved. Somehow, to see him
escorting some glamorous woman would have dimmed her
anticipatory excitement about the party tomorrow.

As Chiara had always been able to burn the candle at both ends, she appeared in the kitchen while Holly was having breakfast the next morning.

'Pour me a tall glass of orange juice, would you? I didn't get to bed till three. But a hot shower will put me right. Then we'll go out and shop till we drop.'

It was while they were having a light lunch at a restaurant where the daytime clientele were women laden with shiny paper carriers bearing names familiar to all readers of *Vogue* that Chiara asked, 'When you met Pierce, did he mention me?'

'Yes. He asked how you were and if you were still single or settled down.'

'That's what he told me I should do. He said I wasn't cut out to be a playgirl. Actually he was very rude. He said that to get to the top as a rich man's darling you had to have brains as well as beauty, and I wasn't clever enough. Well, he was wrong actually. Because while we were down on the Costa, I met someone *really* rich...far richer than Pierce or Eric.'

Holly was appalled. 'Oh, for goodness' sake, Chiara, you're not going to ditch Eric and start yet another of these awful affairs, are you? Pierce was right. What you need is a loving husband and babies. They would make you so much happier than all these horrible older men whose only attraction is their money.'

'Settle down in suburbia with a mortgage and a grizzling toddler in a pushchair? Not likely!' Chiara exclaimed. 'I'm not going to look the way I do now for ever. While I do, I'm making the most of it. And you ain't seen nothing yet, baby, because this guy who gave me the eye on the waterfront at Sotogrande is one of the big-league players. If he fancies me as much as I think he does, I'll have diamonds in every orifice, not just my navel.'

'Lots of men give you the eye. What makes you think he's going to follow it up?'

'Because he sent me a note. It was delivered by hand by one of the stewards on his yacht and it came with a box of chocolates. One of the chocolates was missing. In its place was a huge chunk of aquamarine. I've had it valued. It's worth two thousand pounds. I can't show it to you. It's in a safety-deposit box at the bank. Don't you think that's the most romantic gesture you've ever heard of?'

'What did the note say?'

'Just that he thought I was the most beautiful woman he had ever laid eyes on and he felt sure our paths would cross in the near future.'

In the taxi taking her to the party, Holly knew that she had never looked better. Chiara had done her hair for her, using a styling mousse which added an extra sheen and would hold the ends firmly flipped up.

To go with the Moschino jacket, her stepsister had produced a soft, swingy skirt made of several layers of violet chiffon to tone with the lilac laces. Luckily they both wore size six shoes and Chiara's extensive selection included a pair bought to go with the chiffon skirt, and she even had a pair of lace-topped sheer violet stay-ups.

Holly had never worn stay-ups before and when she was trying them on, wearing rubber gloves to avoid the risk of snagging them, Chiara had said, 'They won't sneak down your legs, I promise you. I wear them all the time. They're much sexier than pantyhose. It gives a guy a real buzz suddenly to feel bare flesh where he thought he was going to feel Lycra.'

'Maybe so, but nobody's going to be putting their hand up *my* skirt tonight,' Holly had said. 'Honestly, Chiara, your relations with men seem to revolve round sex. Don't you ever wish they would grope round your mind for a change?'

'I haven't got that sort of mind. All the things that interest me, men don't want to know about it, and the stuff they drone on about—cars and golf and investments—bore me to death.'

As the taxi sped in the direction of Grosvenor Square, Holly gave a long sigh. She was deeply worried about Chiara. This new affair that she had in prospect with the donor of the aquamarine sounded much deeper water than she had swum in before. But there seemed to be no way of stopping her getting involved if the man concerned wanted her.

Outside Mrs Shintaro's apartment block, a liveried doorman opened the door of the taxi, touching the brim of his cockaded top hat as he said, 'Good evening, miss.'

Holly stepped out and paid the fare with notes taken from a clutch purse of soft glacé kid to match her evening shoes. She would not have bought such high heels for herself and felt slightly awkward in them, but they did flatter her legs, which had never looked longer or more shapely than they did tonight.

As she was about to walk into the building, along the stretch of carpet which led from the kerb to the entrance, protected from rain by an awning, someone pipped the horn of a car.

Turning, she saw Pierce's Jaguar waiting to take the space occupied by her taxi. As she looked through the windscreen he waved to her.

A few minutes later, having handed over his keys to the valet who would park the car for him, Pierce turned to her and said, 'You look wonderful, Holly. I thought you were strictly an open-air, outdoor girl, but tonight you epitomise glamour. What an amusing jacket.'

'Thank you.' She decided not to tell him it was borrowed finery. 'You look very nice yourself.'

He was wearing a pale grey suit with an apricot shirt and tie, all of recognisably superb quality.

He acknowledged her compliment with a slight inclination of his head and then, taking a step back and looking down, said, 'It's a crime to hide those legs in trousers. This is the first time I've seen them.'

Knowing she was starting to blush, she said, 'Skirts aren't practical for gardening.'

Taking her lightly by the elbow, Pierce steered her into the lobby with its luxurious carpet, sofas, silk-shaded lamps and lavish flower arrangements.

There were two lifts, one of them open. In its mirror-lined walls, she caught an unexpected glimpse of him looking down at someone she scarcely recognised as her everyday self.

She had thought he was out of her class, a godlike being she could never hope to ensnare, even though he had claimed to be attracted to her. But now, suddenly, catching sight of their reflections, for the first time she felt it was possible for her to make a small dent in his well-armoured heart. Not for long. Certainly not for ever. But for long enough to make some memories she would always be glad she hadn't missed.

'Although you insisted on coming here by yourself, I refuse to allow you to leave under your own steam,' said Pierce as the lift doors closed. 'Where are you staying?'

'Chiara has a place in Chelsea. I'm spending two nights with her. We're still close. I don't have any contact with her mother and sisters now. Her mother has married again. She's living in Scotland.'

'An obnoxious woman. When Chiara told me who your father was, it was hard to fathom what had possessed him to marry her. But I suppose he thought it was the best thing for you.'

'Yes, and I think she put on an act for him.'

'People of both sexes do that. It's the reason for so many breakups,' Pierce answered drily. 'Whether they're married or only shacked up together, couples suddenly wake up to the fact that the person they're with is someone different from the person they were before the decision to merge. Let's make a pact never to be on our best behaviour with each other.' He smiled. 'That way we'll know where we stand.'

She looked up at him. 'I already know where I stand with you. I'm the Thompson gazelle and you're the leopard. If I don't watch out, you'll have me for dinner.'

Before Pierce had time to reply, the lift doors opened, revealing the landing outside the entrance to the penthouse which tonight stood open, giving a view through the wide hall into Mrs Shintaro's beautiful drawing room.

When she realised what a glittering throng Mrs Shintaro had assembled to meet her grandson, Holly was glad she had Pierce beside her and didn't have to brave the throng of elegant women and distinguished-looking men on her own.

Although she had never been shy, it was nice to feel his hand on the small of her back as they crossed the space between the lift and the wide flight of shallow stairs leading down into the huge room, tonight lit by glittering crystal sconces as well as enormous table lamps making pools of flattering light.

Some people were already relaxing in the groups of sofas and chairs in different parts of the room. Others were standing in groups. Everyone was drinking champagne being served by Japanese waiters in starched white tunics and white gloves.

'Pierce...Holly...' Their hostess had seen them and came hurrying towards them, wearing an exquisite robe of diaphanous dark brown *dévoré* velvet and pearls which could only be real, so beautiful was their soft lustre.

'My dear, you look simply lovely. I knew you would.' Mrs Shintaro embraced her, pressing her cheek to Holly's in a gesture which was as soft as the brush of a moth's wing but far more affectionate than the conventional 'mwah-mwah' kiss.

Lifting her face to receive Pierce's salutation, she said, with a twinkle in her eyes, 'So...there is a détente, as diplomats say when there's an easing of tension between nations which seemed on the brink of strife. I am delighted to see it. Now I want you to meet my treasured grandson, Holly. I have told him how much you liked the Nepalese hand. He's looking forward to meeting a girl with such discriminating taste. Where has he gone to?'

As she started to look round the room, from the opposite direction a young man came through the crowd, making a beeline for Pierce.

Slightly to Holly's surprise, the two men not only clasped hands but gave each other a hug—the kind of embrace which might be exchanged by brothers who had been apart a long time.

She found herself oddly touched by the open affection between them. It threw a new light on Pierce's character. A man who could feel and inspire deep, close friendship must surely be capable of loving? Why his ability to love should be important was something she didn't have time to examine.

As they drew back, the young man turned his attention to Holly. Before his grandmother could present him to her, he said, 'The garden designer, right? I'm Ben Rockland. How do you do, Miss Nicholson.'

'Hello, Ben... Please call me Holly.' As they shook hands, she remembered wondering if he would be good-looking.

He was. She had never seen such a superb example of the mingling of two races. From his American father he had inherited a tall, well-built physique, from his mother, the liquid dark eyes, finely marked brows and jet-black hair of his Japanese ancestors. If she hadn't already met Pierce, she would have thought him the most gorgeous male she had ever seen.

It wasn't until later in the evening that she had a chance to talk to Ben one-to-one. Supper was served in the other parts of the apartment, in a room lined with books and on a glassed-in terrace overlooking some of the city's landmarks, which were picked out by beams of light. Everyone had been given a place at one of the large round tables each seating eight guests.

Holly found herself placed between Ben and an elderly man who introduced himself as an archaeologist. Through the first course she talked to him, and then he turned to his other neighbour and the same thing happened to Ben, leaving them free to concentrate on each other.

He opened the conversation by saying, 'My grandmother has been telling me how she met you. But she said you and Pierce had met before the visit to New Covent Garden.'

'Briefly...a long time ago. You know him much better than I do. You share a passion for mountains, I hear.'

'That's right, and now we're discussing doing an expedition together. Does the name Aconcagua mean anything to you?'

Holly shook her head.

'It's a mountain in Argentina, the highest peak in the Americas. We're going to tackle it in February.'

'Will it be dangerous?'

'Crossing the road can be dangerous,' he answered, smiling. 'It's a difficult summit because of the weather conditions, but it's a mountain you can walk up. There's no serious climbing involved.'

'How long will you be away?'

'Five weeks.'

'It will be an anxious time for your grandmother. She's bound to worry about you.'

'I know. I'm trying to convince her that nothing bad can happen to me while I'm with Pierce, but she still doesn't like the idea. I guess women never do want people they love to take risks, even small ones. But men need a sniff of adventure every so often. Our everyday lives are so tame. We need to live rough for a while, to pit ourselves against the elements.'

'Tell me how you met Pierce.'

'We were both in Nepal, trekking. One day I met up with a small group who weren't experienced trekkers. One of them was showing signs of altitude sickness. I couldn't persuade him he was risking death by pressing on. Then Pierce came by. He has the sort of authority nobody argues with. When the crisis was over, we decided we liked each other. As we were going the same route, we went on together. Not walking together all day, but meeting at each day's end and sleeping in the same lodge. We've been friends ever since. I admire him more than anyone I've ever met.'

'He speaks highly of you,' said Holly. 'Why do you admire him so much? From where I stand he's not especially admirable.'

Yet even as she said it she knew her perspective had altered. She no longer felt hostile towards him. Somehow her feelings had altered. Not at any particular moment. It had happened gradually, subtly.

'Really? But then you don't know him as well as I do.'

'What I do know isn't to his credit.' As soon as the words were out, she wished she had left them unsaid. When Ben looked surprised, she added, 'He had an affair with my stepsister. Then he dropped her.'

She knew as she spoke that she no longer blamed him. There were two sides to every story and perhaps if she knew his side...

'Yes, I've heard he treats women in a way they don't like. But maybe they ask for it. If they're mainly after his money, why should he be nice to them? Did your stepsister love him?'

'No, I don't think she did,' Holly admitted.

'Then she doesn't have much to complain about, does she?' said Ben. 'I don't think he'd hurt anyone who loved him. He's tough, but he isn't cruel. He cares about people more than any man I know.'

'He does?' she said, puzzled. 'In what way?'

Before Ben could answer, the woman on his other side addressed a remark to him. He was obliged to reply. For the rest of the meal they had no further chance to discuss Pierce's character.

When dinner was over, Holly found herself talking to a variety of people, all of them interesting but none of them the person she wanted to be with.

From time to time she saw him talking to other people and she wished she could feel him watching her across the crowded room...like the man and the girl in the song from her parents' favourite musical, the one they had seen on their honeymoon. But Pierce seemed to have forgotten her existence. He never once looked her way.

It was after midnight when the party began to break up. Suddenly Pierce was beside her.

'Are you ready to go?'

'Whenever you are.'

'Let's find Fujiko.'

There were too many guests departing for them to spend long with their hostess. She had her tall grandson beside her.

To Holly's surprise, Ben kissed her goodbye. 'See you soon, I hope.'

Going down in the lift with two other couples. Pierce's replies to her small talk were noticeably monosyllabic. In the lobby they had to wait a few minutes for his car to be brought round.

It was he, not the doorman, who opened the passenger door and watched her tuck the folds of her skirt round her legs.

When the car was in motion, he said, 'I gather you and Ben took to each other.'

'I liked him very much. He told me about your expedition in February and the way you met each other. What does he do for a living? We didn't get to that.'

'By training he's a lawyer, like his father and grandfather. But he doesn't want to practise law. Having an income from a substantial trust fund, he doesn't need to work at all. But he wants to do something useful. The question is— what?'

'Does he have a girlfriend?'

'Not that I know of. I expect he's had lots of girls. He's a good-looking guy. But I don't think there's anyone special. Don't lose your heart to him, Holly.'

'I wasn't planning to, but why the warning?'

'Ben hasn't found his way yet. He's still looking for the right direction. People have to know who they are before they can make important decisions like marriage.'

'You don't believe in love, then? In meeting one's soul mate?'

'I wouldn't say that, but I think it's a pretty rare thing, not something to wait around for, because it may never happen. In general, being happy is something people achieve on their own, not through someone else.'

'Some people say it's because women have careers that so many marriages break down.'

'It's not the career that's the problem. It's the way it's handled,' said Pierce. 'Life is all a question of priorities. But I think I'll expound my theories on that some other time. If you normally get up at six, you must be ready for bed.'

'Strangely, I'm not tired tonight. Usually my light goes out soon after ten. Do you have a lot of late nights?'

'I don't go to many parties. I do tend to read late.'

By now they had reached the street where Chiara lived.

Holly said, 'The flats have their own underground park but it's only accessible to card-holders. As you can see, the street is always fully parked. If you'll drop me off halfway along—'

'I'll double park for a few minutes while I see you safely inside,' he said, in a tone which forbade any argument. 'Street robberies happen all over London these days, not just in seedy areas.'

As he stopped the car, Holly finally nerved herself to say what had been in her mind since they'd left the party.

'Pierce, are you very busy tomorrow? Could you possibly spare half an hour to advise me on something I'm worried about?'

'Of course. What train are you catching?'

'Any train will do. I'm my own boss. I fix my own time-table.'

'To fit you in tomorrow morning would mean reshuffling

a lot of appointments. But I'm not tied up for lunch. Why not come to my place and meet Louisa?'

'Louisa? Oh, yes…your cat. OK, that would be fine.'

He produced a card and wrote his private address on the back of it. Then he walked her to the door of Chiara's flat which had its own entrance along a landscaped walkway under perpetual surveillance by discreetly sited cameras.

Holly wondered if he would kiss her goodnight. Part of her hoped he wouldn't. A kiss from Pierce, even if only on the cheek, the way Ben had kissed her, would be far more disturbing than other men's social kisses.

Another part longed to know what being in his arms would be like.

As she tried to lessen the sound of her heels on the paving, in order not to disturb people who were sleeping, her heart began to beat in slow, suffocating thumps.

CHAPTER FOUR

HAD Holly been on her own, she would have had the key in her hand long before she reached the door. But tonight, protected by the presence of a man whose tall, powerful build would make most muggers think twice, she didn't open her purse until the last moment.

Pierce took the latchkey from her and inserted it quietly in the lock, pushing open the door. Chiara had left the hall light on. Whether she herself was still out there was no way of telling.

'Till tomorrow,' said Pierce, in an undertone. He held out his hand, a slight smile flickering round his mouth.

His fingers and palm were warm, and although his clasp was firm she knew it was nothing like the grip he had exchanged with Ben.

'Thank you for bringing me home. Till tomorrow,' she echoed, looking up at him.

There was a moment when she thought he might be debating whether to kiss her. But perhaps it didn't cross his mind.

Seconds later, he had released her hand and gestured for her to step inside and close the door.

Next morning she overslept. Troubled thoughts had kept her awake for a long time. Chiara was eating muesli and flipping through *The Tatler*, an upmarket glossy aimed at people in the social swim, or those who admired and envied them.

'I'm in for the third month running,' she announced on a note of triumph, showing Holly a picture of herself revealing more cleavage than anyone else on the same page.

'Congratulations.' Holly opened the fridge and took out a carton of orange juice.

'How was the party?' asked Chiara.

'Good...very good.'

'Who brought you home?'

'Pierce.'

'Did he know you were staying with me?'

'Yes.'

'Did you ask him in for a nightcap?'

'No.'

'Why not? Were you afraid he'd make a pass?'

'Not asking him in avoided that possibility.'

'Maybe he's between girlfriends and wouldn't mind seeing me again,' said Chiara.

'Would you like the satisfaction of telling him to get lost?'

'I might...or I might let him pick up where we left off.'

'I don't understand you, Chiara. Don't you have *any* scruples? Yesterday you were talking about ditching Eric for this man who gave you the aquamarine, and now you're interested in Pierce. How can this sort of life possibly lead to happiness?'

'I'm not like you, Holly. You're a fanatical idealist. You want life to be like a fairy story. It isn't and never was. Who do you know who's living happily ever after? Nobody. OK, your parents might have done, but only *might*. You can't say for certain because your mother died before the gloss had worn off.'

Holly sighed. It was no use arguing. They saw life from different perspectives, hers perhaps as extreme as Chiara's.

When Pierce himself opened his door to her, he was still in the dark blue suit of the kind she associated with boardrooms and the corridors of power.

'Come in. It's Hooper's day off so I'm having something sent round from a restaurant.'

'Oh, dear...I hope I'm not putting you to a lot of trouble. It's just that you're the only person who has the know-how to advise on the situation I'm bothered about.'

'I'm flattered to be asked,' he said, standing by to take her raincoat. 'It shows how far we've advanced since that morning at New Covent Garden.'

After hanging her coat in a cupboard, he led the way to a huge double-cube room with an enormous north window.

'Was this an artist's studio?' Holly asked, gazing round.

'You've got it in one. Nearly a hundred years ago, this was the studio of a very distinguished artist who specialised in paintings of domestic life in Ancient Rome. That way he gave an air of respectability to pictures which, by the standards of the day, were extremely erotic. Scantily dressed Roman maidens, attended by semi-nude slaves, lolling around on the steps of marble bathing pools...that sort of thing. What will you drink? Vodka and tonic?'

'Yes, please.'

While Pierce went to a side table set with rows of bottles and glasses, Holly wandered around, admiring the profusion of Oriental rugs laid almost edge-to-edge on the parquet floor and the massive expanses of books lining sections of the walls.

Suddenly she became aware of a pair of large golden-green eyes, black-rimmed as if with kohl, watching her from the depths of a large armchair.

'Oh...you must be Louisa,' Holly said, smiling.

The cat twitched large tufted ears, her expression enigmatic. With slow deliberation, she uncurled from her resting position, stretching each leg in turn. Then she leapt lightly to the floor where she sat down on her hind legs and gave a desultory lick to one upraised front paw.

Holly went down on her haunches, making small pursed-lip noises and rubbing her fingers together in a gesture of invitation.

After some thought, Louisa walkèd slowly towards her. In colour, her coat was not dissimilar from Parson's, but much shaggier, with a thick pale grey ruff and a long tapered tail covered with flowing hair.

Two yards from Holly's outstretched hand, she veered in a different direction.

'Your cat has just cut me dead,' said Holly, rising to her feet. Pierce was still fixing their drinks and hadn't witnessed the snub.

'She takes time to make up her mind about people,' he said as he brought the drinks to where she was standing. 'Some of my oldest friends are still trying to ingratiate themselves with Louisa. She's a very discriminating pussycat. Perhaps she senses that you have reservations about me.'

'Not as many as I had or I shouldn't be here.' Holly took the glass he offered. 'Thank you. Happy landings!'

'Is that what your father used to say?'

'Yes. How did you guess?'

'Male intuition. We have it too, you know. Not as finely tuned as female intuition, perhaps. But we do have it.'

'I'm sure you do. Sometimes I feel you can see straight through me,' Holly said, with impulsive candour.

'On the contrary, I spent a long time pondering this problem you want my advice on, but I've no idea what it is.

Let's make ourselves comfortable and you can tell me all about it.'

He led the way to a sofa designed for the comfort of people his size. Before sitting down, he moved some cushions from the centre to the end where she would be sitting to make it more comfortable for her.

Holly took a swig of her drink. She had been rehearsing what to say all the way here, but still found it difficult to know where to start.

'If a man and a girl exchanged looks in a public place, and shortly afterwards the girl received a very expensive jewel from him, what would your reaction be?' she asked.

For the first time since they had renewed their acquaintance, Pierce's grey eyes took on the cold look she remembered from their first meeting five years ago. His whole face seemed to harden. As he had no superfluous flesh on his cheeks and neck, it was easy to see the movements of the muscles under the closely shaven brown skin. Right now he was clenching his teeth, causing knots of sinew to form at the angles of his jaw.

'Have you ever done that yourself…wooed a woman you wanted with a fabulous gift?' she asked.

'Certainly not!' he said curtly. 'My only extravagant gestures have been for services rendered.'

The statement made Holly wince. She realised suddenly that Pierce's attitude to sex was as deeply distasteful to her as Chiara's. He looked a superior being. Why couldn't he act like one?

'What was this expensive jewel?' Pierce asked.

'A two-thousand-pound aquamarine. It came in a box of chocolates. It was the size of a chocolate…huge. Like a chunk of crystallised sea-water.'

'How do you know what it cost? Did it have the receipt with it?'

'Chiara took it to a jeweller. She couldn't believe it was real. But he said it was...a stone of the finest quality.'

Pierce's expression changed. 'It was sent to Chiara...not you?'

'Well, of course. Nobody would send *me* something like that,' Holly said, with a wry smile. 'I'd be lucky even to get the handmade chocolates.'

'You underestimate yourself,' Pierce said brusquely. 'When and where did this happen, and what do you know about the man who gave Chiara the aquamarine?'

Holly told him all she knew. 'What terrifies me is that he may be a criminal,' she said, frowning. 'It's a well-known fact that there are some very shady people living on the Costa del Sol. People involved with the Mafia and all kinds of sinister rackets.'

'Does she know the name of his yacht?' Pierce asked.

'No. I asked her that. My first thought was that the only person able to afford such an extravagant gesture would be an Arab prince. A lot of them do have villas and luxury yachts on the Costa del Sol, I believe.'

'Yes, they do,' Pierce agreed. 'I've been there and seen them playing for high stakes in casinos and at private parties. Did this guy look like an Arab?'

'He had black hair and eyes and an olive skin, but so do Spaniards and South Americans.'

'Did you ask her if he had a beard?'

'No, I didn't think of that. Do most Arabs have beards?'

'A lot of them do...not all. It's a pity she didn't notice the name of the boat. With that, we could have run an extensive check on him. Without anything to go on, we're stymied. We can only wait to see if he follows it up and then hope to get some kind of lead on him.'

He shifted his position, moving along the sofa until he was close enough to put his hand over her free hand. 'Don't fret about it, Holly. I don't think it's very likely that Chiara is going to wind up a prisoner in a harem or the mistress of a Mafia boss. You're looking at the worst scenario.' He gave her a long thoughtful look. 'It's not impossible this guy took one look at Chiara and fell in love with her. It can happen like that...so they say.'

'I can't believe that you, of all people, attach much weight to *that* scenario.'

'Why d'you say "you, of all people"? If you prick me, do I not bleed? If you tickle me, do I not laugh? If you poison me, do I not die?'

He was misquoting Shylock in Shakespeare's *The Merchant of Venice*, and it pleased her that he assumed she was as well read as he.

'Of course...but how many men experience love at first sight? One in a thousand, I should think. It seems to happen to women more often than it does to men, and even then often it's only an infatuation...not the real thing.'

Pierce took his hand from hers but didn't move back to the other end of the sofa. 'Perhaps. One thing is certain; it wasn't a *coup de foudre* on Chiara's side,' he said sardonically. 'Your stepsister would never give up everything for love. I sometimes wonder if any of your generation of women would. You're a new breed. Love is no longer your whole existence the way it used to be. Now you think about love the way men do, as a thing apart, to be weighed and measured against life's other prizes.'

'Perhaps some of us do,' said Holly. 'But not all of us. A lot of life's prizes are still out of reach for most women. If you added up all the successful career women and other female achievers, they'd still be a tiny fraction of the entire sex. There are thousands of women in the world who are literally slaves, for heaven's sake.'

'Men too...slaves of poverty. Save your feminist polemics for someone else, Holly. I know more about the world's underclasses than you might imagine.' His dark eyebrows drew together. 'Too damn much,' he said, in a harsh voice.

Holly wondered what he meant. Before she could ask, a bell rang.

'That'll be our food arriving. Stay and finish your drink. I'll call you when lunch is served.'

He sprang up and strode off towards a door in the far corner of the room.

When he had gone, she rose from the sofa and wandered about, looking at his pictures and possessions. Had she been shown this room before meeting its owner, she would have formed a very different impression from the one fixed in her mind by their first encounter at her stepmother's party.

Everything here indicated a man whose inclinations were intellectual and artistic rather than solely sybaritic. His library was as wide-ranging as her father's had been, with many books on philosophy and history that she had seen before on Professor Nicholson's shelves.

After his death, his second wife had lost no time in clearing his study and having the room redecorated. Holly had come home from secretarial college to find his books had been sold to a second-hand dealer. It had been a betrayal of trust she still couldn't bear to think about. After that, as soon as she'd been able to she had left the house which was no longer home to her, to stand on her own feet.

Taking a well-worn leather-bound copy of *An Introduction to Kant's Ethics* from the shelf, she opened it, expecting to see Pierce's signature on the flyleaf. Instead, to her amazement, she found herself looking at her father's book-plate with his name written in ink under the printed '*Ex Libris*'.

Overcome with excitement, she ran to the door in the corner, calling, 'Pierce...Pierce...where are you?'

He appeared in another doorway at the end of a passage. 'Here I am. What's the matter?'

'Where did you get this book?'

'What is it?'

'*Kant's Ethics.*'

Like her father, he obviously knew every book in his possession. 'A dealer I know rang up and said he'd bought a collection of books which might interest me. That was one of them. Why?'

'Because it belonged to my father. Look, here's his book-plate.' She thrust the book at him. 'All these years I've been wondering where his books were...imagining them scattered in houses all over the country. I never go past a second-hand bookshop without hoping to find one and buy it back. And the first time I've ever seen one is here, in your house. It's incredible.'

'P.J. Nicholson... Good Lord, was he your father? I didn't make the connection. I suppose, never having met him, it didn't occur to me that the previous owner of this book could be Chiara's stepfather, even though she had mentioned he was "boringly brainy", as she put it.'

'Can you remember how many of his books you bought? Several...a dozen...more than that?'

'About a hundred, as far as I can remember. Tell you what, after lunch why don't you pick out as many as you can carry and take them back with you?'

'Oh, no, I couldn't do that. They belong to you now. It's just so lovely to know where they are...that they've found a good home.'

'That's a change of tune,' he said drily. 'You didn't feel that way the second time we met.'

'Well, I do now. I'm beginning to think I misjudged you.

I'm not saying I think it was right to make Chiara your mistress, but it wasn't as bad as it seemed to me at the time.'

They ate lunch at a small fruitwood table in a corner of the studio, with Louisa watching from the arm of a nearby sofa.

Pierce did not feed her titbits but occasionally glanced in her direction with an affectionate look which she returned with a blink of her beautiful eyes. Holly wondered if, on evenings when he wasn't out, she lay on his lap, being gently caressed by one of his long, tanned hands while the other turned the pages of a book.

'How did you spend this morning?' he asked.

'I didn't do very much. I was up later than usual. I packed my things and then I went out and found a nice card for my thank-you note to Mrs Shintaro. Then I roughed out my note and rewrote it in my best handwriting. Then I posted it, and then I came here.'

'She'll be pleased you took the trouble to write. Most people only ring up. Some don't bother to do that. Being punctilious herself, Fujiko sets store in the traditional forms of politeness. In the past, some of Ben's girlfriends have upset her with their offhand manners. Her own marriage was *o miai* which means arranged by her parents. An *o miai* marriage isn't a matter of compulsion. It's a bringing together of people who seem to their parents or friends to have plenty in common. Fujiko and her husband were so compatible that not long after their marriage they were as much in love as any Western couple.'

'Does she want to arrange Ben's marriage?'

'She'd like to see him marry a Japanese girl. But as Fujiko herself is now very westernised and spends more time in London and New York than in her own country, I think it's unlikely Ben will ever return to his ancestral roots.'

After a pause he added, 'One of the books which was your father's is a history of the Second World War and its aftermath. That war left hundreds of thousands of what were called "displaced persons". They could never go back to where they had lived before, but they were never really at home where they ended up when it was over. Unlike the DPs, Fujiko and Ben have money and status. But in a sense they are both displaced persons, suspended between two cultures and not quite at home in either.'

'Will you always live in England?' she asked. 'Have you transplanted completely?'

'I think so, but always is a long time. Who knows? When I'm an old man, my wife and I might decide we would rather spend this time of year in a warmer climate. I shouldn't want to retire to the Costa del Sol, but I have friends who live in the mountains behind that coast. They're not far from an international airport but the way of life in their village dates back to a time long before flight was dreamed possible. It's a lovely place...very peaceful. I can visualise living there.'

'You are going to marry one day, then?'

'That was never in doubt.' Today they were drinking wine and he broke off to top up their glasses. 'But until my own life was properly organised, it would have been premature to look for a wife.'

'You make a wife sound like something that can be shopped for. I thought, like husbands, they cropped up when least expected.'

'So they may, but the circumstances have to be propitious. For instance, the first time we met neither of us was ready for marriage. You were too young and I had problems with my working life. Let's assume I had never met Chiara but had come to the party as somebody's house guest. On the premise that we had taken one look at each other and thought, This is it, do you think it would have worked out?'

It was such a strange thing to say that Holly was momentarily nonplussed.

As she floundered for a reply, Pierce answered for her. 'It wouldn't have got off the ground. But now the situation is different. We both of us know who we are and where we're heading. If I were to suggest that we pooled our resources, and if you were to agree, we'd stand a good chance of becoming one of those ideal couples whom everyone wants to emulate but very few do.'

Unable to meet the teasing gleam in his eyes, Holly looked down at her plate, at what remained of a salmon steak which had followed a first course of Chinese prawns on a bed of green tagliatelle.

'Without being in love to begin with?' Her mouth felt curiously dry.

'What does "being in love" mean to you? Define it for me.'

'Being very strongly attracted...liking a person's mind as well as their physical looks...trusting them...wanting to be with them always...feeling that life without them would be an endless desert...' With a gesture expressing the impossibility of putting such a complex emotion into words, she gave up.

'I would disagree with that last bit,' said Pierce. 'Life is never or rarely a desert. Happiness shouldn't depend on being with another person. I'd go as far as to say you can only love someone else if you love and are satisfied with the life you're leading before they show up. It's all right to feel something's missing...that there's another dimension that will make it all even better. But I'd only marry a girl who had got her own act together...as, for example, you have.'

'Well, yes, that makes sense,' said Holly. 'The only thing is, you can't always go by appearances. When you came to that party with Chiara, you seemed to have life on a string. Now you say that was not so.'

'I was making a lot of money, but I didn't feel what I was doing served any useful purpose other than making me richer. I needed a greater challenge and certain intangible rewards. Now, by redirecting my energies, I have both.'

At this point the telephone rang. Pierce excused himself to answer it.

Holly, whose mobile phone had revolutionised her life, was a little surprised that he didn't keep one within arm's reach but went to a jacked-in set at the far end of the room.

She was wondering what form the redirection of his career had taken, and intending to ask him, when after a very brief chat with the person on the line he came back.

'I'm sorry, Holly. I'm going to have to cut this short. I need to get back to my office. I was hoping to take you to the station, but you'll have to call a taxi. This is the number to ring.' He had already written it down on a page from a pad by the telephone. 'But stay and finish your lunch. There's no need for you to rush off because I have to. Maybe if I'm not around, Louisa will unbend and make friends with you.'

'But what about locking up?' she said anxiously. 'Are there complicated burglar alarms which need to be set?'

'No, it's all completely automatic. You don't have to worry about a thing...except the calories in the pudding,' he said, with a smile. 'Which, judging by the shape you revealed last night, isn't a problem for you anyway.'

As she rose from her chair, he added, 'About the problem

with Chiara— I'll give it some thought and call you…
possibly tonight.'

'Thank you for lunch, Pierce—' she began.

'My pleasure. I only wish I didn't have to dash off. We
must do it again…very soon.'

He put his hands on her shoulders and bent to kiss her
on both cheeks.

Seconds later, while she was still in a whirl from the
touch of his lips on her face, he was on his way to the front
door.

Holly's train journey back to Norfolk seemed to pass in a
flash, her thoughts being in such a flurry of astonishment,
joy and apprehension.

How could she be in love with a man who, only a short
time ago, had been the one person on earth she heartily
detested? Could it be, could it *possibly* be that his conversation at lunch meant that he was beginning to feel she was
someone special, someone different from all his girlfriends—someone he could come to love?

Suddenly, to be loved by Pierce was more important than
anything she had ever set her heart on since she'd been a
little girl longing to find that one of the parcels under the
Christmas tree had a camera in it.

Since then there had been many other things she had
wanted, including the prize which had given her career such
a boost. But none had been even fractionally as important
as this. On this her whole life depended. For, if he didn't
want her, how could she ever make do with anyone else?
It had to be Pierce or no one.

The instant his hard male cheek had brushed hers and
she'd felt the slight movement of his lips in what, outwardly, had had no more significance than Ben's kiss the
night before, or a thousand other social kisses, her mind

had at last acknowledged what her heart had known for a long time.

She had been in love with Pierce Sutherland since he'd first walked into her life. That was the real reason she had been so upset when he'd ditched Chiara: the man she had wanted to idolise had proved to have feet of clay and her nineteen-year-old heart, unable to come to terms with that, had taken refuge in pretending to loathe him.

After making herself a light supper and giving Parson his favourite evening meal—sardines in tomato sauce—she went to bed early.

She was reading the current issue of *The Garden*, with Parson curled on the outside of the old patchwork quilt she had found in a junk shop, when the telephone rang.

'Hello?'

'It's Pierce. I'm sorry I had to desert you.'

'It didn't matter. It was good of you to see me in the first place.'

'Nonsense. I wanted to see you. Lunching with you was a lot more enjoyable than having a sandwich at my desk. Listen, tomorrow I have to go overseas for a few days. I'm not sure when I'll be back, but as soon as I am I'll call you and we'll pick up where we left off. Also something came up this afternoon which I need to consult you about. I won't go into it now, except to say that it's right up your alley.'

'Something to do with gardens?'

'It's too complicated to explain on the telephone. Take care of yourself, Green Fingers.'

'You too. Where are you going?'

'Africa. I have to say goodnight now.'

'Goodnight, Pierce...' she waited until he had cut the connection before adding softly, 'Darling.'

*   *   *

The day after Pierce's departure two nice things happened, followed by something upsetting.

Holly was having her breakfast when Mrs Shintaro called to say she had a long-standing invitation to a golden-wedding lunch party at the country home of some old friends she had met when they and her husband, then a young diplomat, had been *en poste* in Rio de Janeiro many years ago. As their house was only ten miles from where Holly was living, and Ben was taking the place of her usual driver, she wondered if Holly would take him under her wing for a few hours until it was time for him to collect her for the journey back to London.

Holly agreed with alacrity, feeling sure that Ben would be able to explain many things she wanted to know about Pierce, as well as clarifying the remark he had made during supper at his grandmother's party.

Unfortunately it was a horrible day for their drive, with rain sloshing down and no sign of a break in the clouds. As she wasn't able to work outside, she spent the morning preparing a hot lunch. While she was cooking, the postman delivered a large padded bag which proved to contain half a dozen of her father's books.

Pierce had written in handwriting as bold and incisive as his personality:

I've always believed that we make our own destinies, but now I'm beginning to wonder if there's something in fate after all. The African trip is a nuisance just now but can't be avoided. Keep a space for me in your diary in the early part of next week. It will be a professional assignment with personal intervals.

She was still pondering what the last sentence might mean when Ben arrived, wearing a leather aviator's jacket over a coral sweater which set off his colouring.

'This is very kind of you, Holly. I hope I'm not disrupting your life too much by descending on you this way. The people my grandmother's lunching with would have fitted me in, but I would have felt like an interloper. They're all around sixty or seventy. Lunching with you will be a lot more fun.'

'You're not disrupting anything,' Holly assured him. 'Because of the heavy rain I'd switched my schedule around to make this my day for house-cleaning. Now the chores are done, the rest of the day is free. If it should clear up later I'll take you to see the garden I'm working on, but I've just heard a radio forecast and I think we're going to be house-bound.'

Ben had run down the garden path with a yachtsman's bright yellow waterproof worn like a cloak over his sheepskin-lined leather jacket. Now, from its capacious pockets, he began to take various packages.

'In Japan it's the custom to take one's hostess a present,' he said. 'As I didn't know I was coming until this morning, I had to shop in a hurry. These are not what, given more time, I would have chosen for you, but they may come in useful.'

As she unwrapped his offerings, Holly found he had paid a flying visit to the grocery department of Fortnum & Mason, one of London's most famous stores, and selected a range of their special delicacies.

'They all look delicious…thank you. Let me hang up your coats… Oh, this is Parson, my cat,' she added as he, hearing an unfamiliar voice, came through from the kitchen to inspect the visitor.

Ben went down on his haunches. 'Hi, Parson. You're a fine fellow.' He stroked the tabby's broad head and tickled him under one ear, setting off Parson's deepest, most friendly purr.

'I wish I'd had that effect on Louisa, Pierce's cat,' said Holly, watching them making friends. 'She was very uppity with me. Have you managed to win her over?'

'She's OK with guys but jealous of women,' said Ben, standing up. 'A long time ago, Pierce had a girlfriend who was allergic to cats and Louisa had to be shut in the kitchen whenever she was around. I think she was deeply offended and has never got over it. Forgive me if I'm being too nosy, but are you and Pierce starting something?'

Holly was disconcerted. 'What makes you think we might be?'

'My grandmother told me that when she gave you a ride back from New Covent Garden you were reacting to each other so strongly that she thought the atmosphere was about to ignite.'

'That was because he was then at the top of my hate list,' said Holly. 'I don't feel that way about him now, but our friendship is still very new. What did you mean when you said he cared about people more than anyone you knew?'

'Pierce has been fighting a battle against corruption in the developing countries,' said Ben. 'He realised how much aid from taxpayers in the rich countries was never reaching the people it was intended to help and began a campaign to change that. Now he's set up an organisation, of which he is the dynamo, that's already made a big difference to the situation worldwide. Of course it's also made him a lot of powerful enemies among the people who were making fortunes for themselves by siphoning off money and relief supplies. But I don't think he's as much at risk now as he was in the early days. If they could have got rid of him then, the whole project might have foundered.'

'You mean they might have killed him?' Holly asked, shaken.

'Oh, sure. If you were lining your pockets from the bottomless pit of international aid, how would you feel about a guy who was trying to stop you? They hated his guts and they were the kind of people whose enemies wind up feeding the crocodiles or worse.'

'Is he in danger now…on this trip to Africa?' she asked.

'Probably not. The organisation he founded is too solidly based to fall apart at this stage. There would be no point in wiping him out. Don't worry: he can look after himself. He's not a guy who ever takes stupid risks. He might take a calculated chance sometimes, but he doesn't make careless mistakes. You don't need to lose any sleep about him.'

'At the moment Pierce and I are just friends,' Holly said pointedly. 'The only thing that keeps me awake at night is wondering where my next commission is coming from.'

But, later, after Ben had left to pick up his grandmother, she knew that what she had told him wasn't true. She *would* be anxious about Pierce until she knew he was safely back in London.

She had put some more logs on the fire and was sitting, with Parson curled on her lap, listening to his rhythmic purr and the sound of the rising wind and rain beating on the curtained windows, when the telephone rang.

Irrationally hoping it might be a call from somewhere in Africa, Holly was surprised to hear her stepsister saying angrily, 'What the hell do you mean by telling Pierce what I told you? It's none of his damn business…or yours, come to that. You've no right to go shooting your mouth off about my private affairs. And he's got no bloody right to come roaring round here, telling me how to run my life.'

'When did he come to see you?' Holly asked, bewildered and shocked by the rage in her stepsister's voice.

'Last night. Barged in here as if he owned the place and read me the Riot Act about behaving recklessly and being a worry to you. I tried to keep him out, but anyone would have thought it was a police raid the way he stormed in and started hectoring me. The worst of it was that Eric was in the bedroom. Naturally he wanted to know what the hell was going on.'

'Did Pierce tell him?'

'He didn't need to. He'd already said enough for Eric to guess that something was up. By the time Pierce had gone, he was spoiling for a row. I lost my temper and shouted back at him. Eventually he slammed out. The chances are, I'll never see him again...and all because you blabbed to Pierce about something that doesn't concern either one of you.'

In the moment before she slammed the phone down, Holly heard her bursting into noisy tears.

CHAPTER FIVE

THIRTY seconds later Holly rang Chiara's number, only to hear a recorded answering-machine message.

After the tone, she said, 'Chiara, I had no idea Pierce intended to deal with this business as he did. Truly I didn't. But I can't deny that I did consult him. He seemed the only person I could turn to for advice. I was worried about you...seriously worried. Bad things can happen to girls who get involved with men they know nothing about. I'm sorry if the way Pierce handled it has made things difficult with Eric, but I have to say this isn't Pierce's fault or mine. It's yours...for two-timing Eric...or at least being prepared to ditch him if a better offer turns up.

'If I didn't love you, I wouldn't care what you did. But I can't bear to see you going down this dangerous road which could end in a sordid story in one of the tabloids. You've never been very good at facing unpleasant facts and you won't get any sensible advice from your mother. Pierce knows the world better than either of us. Please think over what he said to you. Please don't shut me out of your life. I'm not going to sleep a wink unless you call back.'

Chiara didn't call back, nor did Holly really expect her to. After the quarrels of their childhood and teen years, her stepsister had invariably sulked—a trait she had learned from her mother, who had used the same technique with her second husband if he'd made what she'd call 'a fuss' about her extravagance.

It had been an unhappy marriage on every level and eventually they had slept in separate rooms, not only, Holly suspected, because of her father's heart condition but because the intimacy of sharing a bed had become distasteful to them both.

She had never been able to understand how her father could have contemplated a sexual relationship with Nora in the first place. But, of course, she had seen her stepmother through the eyes of a child who would have resented anyone usurping her natural mother.

When she had been old enough to view the situation sensibly, she had realised that at the time of the marriage Nora must have been almost as lovely as Chiara was now. Was it surprising that her father, desperately lonely and needing someone to care for his motherless daughter, had been seduced by Nora's alluring looks and the winning ways she could adopt when it suited her?

Holly didn't stay awake all night, but her restless tossings and turnings caused Parson to remove himself from his preferred position against the small of her back and station himself near the footboard of the pine double bed, a reproduction of a French farmhouse bed.

It was Pierce's handling of the matter which had been on her mind during the night and still preoccupied her the next morning as she gave Parson his breakfast before attending to her own.

She wanted very much to believe that Pierce's impetuous action, so different from the cool-headed behaviour she would have expected of him, had been prompted by feelings warmer than mere friendship. Could it be—oh, please let it be!—that he was beginning to feel the same way about her as she did about him?

She had eaten her muesli and was peeling a couple of satsumas when the telephone rang.

'Hello?'

'It's me,' said Chiara. 'I've cooled down a bit since last night. I'm still furious with you, but I suppose you meant well.'

To Holly's amazement, she heard her stepsister giggle. 'I've just had a huge basket of flowers by special delivery. They're from Eric. The note says he's sorry he shouted and swore at me last night. He wants to come round this morning and take me shopping. Reading between the lines, he's going to buy me something bigger and better than an aquamarine. There's a bracelet in a shop in Bond Street I rather fancy. It'll cost him an arm and a leg, but why not? He can afford it.'

'Does that mean you're going to stay with him and give the aquamarine back when the other man makes contact with you?'

'Not likely! Why would I do that? Honestly, Hol, your ideas are so Victorian, it isn't true. I suppose it's because you only earn peanuts yourself and you and whoever you marry will never have any serious spending power. But the men I know are in a different league. A diamond bracelet to them is like a packet of seeds to you.'

Probably because she was tired, Holly was on a short fuse. She said crisply, 'Personally, I'd rather have an inexpensive engagement ring from a man who loved me and wanted to marry me than a million pounds' worth of jewels from a lot of randy older men to whom I was nothing more than a sex object. Excuse me, I have to go and earn another peanut.'

She rang off.

The days that followed seemed endless. Holly scoured the columns of *The Times*, fearful of finding a paragraph about the body of an unidentified European male being found in mysterious circumstances in some part of Africa. That she didn't even know which part of that vast continent he was in somehow increased her anxiety.

Every time the telephone rang, her heart seemed to stop beating until the caller identified himself.

In between times she went over every word Pierce had said to her, looking for nuances she might have missed the first time.

When, at last, he did ring it was after she had turned out the light and was lying awake, thinking about him.

Thinking it might be Chiara, with whom she hadn't spoken since the peanuts conversation, she let it ring several times before picking up the receiver.

'Hello?'

'It's Pierce. How are you?'

Holly shot into a sitting position, disturbing Parson, who stopped his drowsy purring and gave a mew of displeasure.

'Pierce! Where are you? Are you all right?'

'I got home five minutes ago. I'm fine. What about you?'

'Fine...great.' The fact that he had called her so soon after his arrival made her spirits soar. 'How was your trip?'

'Successful, but I'm glad it's over. How soon can you give me that day I asked you to keep free?'

'As soon as you wish.'

'Tomorrow?'

'Yes, if you like.'

'Tomorrow it is. I'll pick you up about nine.' He explained where the airfield was and then added, 'Tell that cat of yours he may have to fend for himself for twelve hours...possibly overnight.'

'Why overnight?'

'Because we'll be going to Devon and at this time of

year weather conditions can worsen quite rapidly. We might need to spend the night locally.'

'OK, I'll make some contingency arrangements.'

'Until tomorrow.' Pierce rang off.

The following morning, Holly had her first experience of flying in a helicopter. She had heard they were difficult to handle, but Pierce seemed to have no problem in keeping the machine smoothly on course for their destination.

England, seen from a much lower altitude than she had flown at before, presented a fascinating patchwork of fields, villages, woods, major and minor roads, grand and less grand country houses, private swimming pools, flooded quarries and what he told her were fish farms.

In a fraction of the time it would have taken to get there by road or rail, they arrived on the other side of England, landing at a small private airfield where Pierce had arranged for a car and a driver to be waiting. A basket containing coffee and sandwiches had also been laid on, and Holly began to realise how relaxed and enjoyable journeys could be when masterminded by a man with unlimited resources.

It was during this stage of the journey that he finally disclosed the purpose of the trip.

'For a couple of years I've had one of the best estate agencies looking for a country place for me,' he explained. 'I've visited dozens of houses all over England but none of them had that special something about them you want in a place you're hoping to live in for the rest of your life and hand on to your children. The house we're going to see this morning came on the market a month ago. I've already been over it twice. Now I'd like to have your opinion of it.'

'But Pierce, I don't know about houses. I only know

about gardens...and there are people far more expert than myself whom you could consult.'

'Perhaps, but experts tend to be older rather than younger and I want to know how the house strikes someone of your age. Is it a white elephant which ought to be left to moulder into a picturesque ruin, or is it a dream waiting to be realised?'

'Why has it come on the market?'

'The old man who owned it died. He was in his nineties and very short of money. The place has been badly neglected for a couple of decades. He did have descendants, but none of them wants it. Apparently his sons and daughters were all adventurous, as he was himself in his youth, and they settled in places like New Zealand and Costa Rica. They and their children have rooted in other countries and don't want to be transplanted. So the house is up for grabs; only, it's so far gone that most buyers don't bother to view it, or take one look and get back in their cars.'

By this time Holly had grasped why he had laid on a driver. Clearly the house was well off the beaten track, reached by a labyrinth of largely unsignposted lanes in which anyone unfamiliar with the area would easily lose their way.

'It's a long way from the nearest railway station and over an hour from the motorway. For anyone work-based in London the only practical transport is by air,' Pierce went on. 'However, at the moment the grounds are in such a shambles, there's nowhere to land. Anyway I wanted you to see it from the ground. We're nearly there now. The main gate is round the next corner.'

The iron gates which came into view a few moments later had, judging by their design, been beautifully wrought by a master craftsman at least two hundred years ago. Now, flanked by ornamental lodges not large enough to be called cottages, the gates were long overdue for a fresh coat of paint. Chained together and padlocked, they barred the way to a wide drive lined with ancient beeches, their massive branches now leafless.

As the driver got out to unlock and open the gates, Holly had a curious feeling that she had seen this gateway before. Yet she knew she couldn't have done so because she had never set foot in Devon.

The meadows on either side of the drive were being grazed by sheep, those near the fences raising their heads to stare impassively at the passing car.

Then, as it rounded a bend, the house came into view, and again she had an uncannily strong sensation of *déjà vu*.

'I wonder if it's been featured in *Country Life*?' she said, half to herself. 'It seems so familiar. What is it called, this house?'

'Not something you would expect in this part of the world,' said Pierce. 'It was built in 1815 by a colonel who'd been invalided out of Wellington's army. He'd been badly wounded in some of the fiercest fighting of the Peninsular campaign. Like many veterans of that war, he called his house after a battle he'd fought in. Talavera. It's an odd name to find in the wilds of Devon, isn't it?' Something in her expression made him ask, 'What's the matter?'

'Nothing. It's just that Talavera is a very familiar name to me.'

'How come? Did you do the Peninsular War in your history lessons at school?'

'No, it was reading novels set in the Regency, not history lessons, which taught me about that period. But that's not why the name Talavera strikes a chord. One of my favourite vases for very small flowers like primroses and violets is a little yellow pottery jar. On the bottom is written, in

Spanish, "Made by hand—Talavera." I found it in a charity shop. I suppose the previous owner brought it back from Spain as a souvenir.'

By now the car had drawn up in front of the house and the driver was opening the rear door on Pierce's side. He sprang out, turning to offer his hand to Holly.

Even though most of her attention was focused on the house they had come to see, the contact with his palm and fingers sent a frisson of pleasure feathering along her nerves.

'The style is called Picturesque Gothic,' said Pierce as they stood side by side, looking at the façade of a substantial mansion which, in spite of its size, had a cosy, almost cottagey air about it. Perhaps this came from the windows with their pointed-arch glazing bars, or from the mock battlements along the roof-line and the ornamental turrets at each angle of the building.

'The central block was built first and then the wings added on as the family expanded,' said Pierce.

The driver, who was evidently under instructions from the Devon office of Pierce's estate agents, was unlocking the front door for them.

As she entered the hall, lit by sunlight streaming through French windows at the far end and through a large window at the turn of the graceful staircase, Holly was aware that the house was in dire disrepair. Yet instantly, in her mind's eye, she could see it as it had once been and could be again.

As Pierce showed her round, no one with eyes in their head could have ignored the evidence of galloping decay. In the small bathroom part of the sprung floor had collapsed. In the attics, a score of buckets were positioned to catch drips from holes in the roof.

'Have you worked out what it would cost to put it in order?' she asked him.

'Only roughly, but it's a daunting amount,' he said, his mouth wry. 'Don't tell me what you think of it until we've looked round the grounds.'

To Holly, neglected gardens had a beauty all their own. When they came to the walled kitchen garden, it evoked powerful memories of sitting in the circle of her father's arm while he read her the stories he had loved as a small boy, his first favourites being the little books by Beatrix Potter about families of rabbits, and mice who could do fine embroidery.

It was in a corner of the kitchen garden that Pierce turned to her and said, 'Do you think I'm mad even to contemplate taking it on?'

Above a serpentine wall of mellow old bricks could be seen the chimneypots of the house and the tops of many fine trees.

'I don't think I should say what I think,' she said slowly. 'It's a purely emotional reaction, completely divorced from common sense.'

'Are you saying that you like Talavera?'

'I feel the same way about it as I did about my yellow pot. That was love at first sight and so is this,' she admitted. 'If I had the money—which I haven't—I could spend the rest of my life putting Talavera to rights. It may be falling to bits, but for me it has everything a house should have. Atmosphere...charm...character...all those intangible factors which have nothing to do with practicality and everything to do with being happy in a place.'

Pierce turned away and took a few paces along the weed-strewn brick path. Then, returning to where she was standing, he said, 'I feel the same way. My head tells me I must be mad. My heart says otherwise. I *do* have the means to do it, but I wanted someone whose judgement I value to tip the balance for me.'

'I can't think why you should value my judgement. What I know about high finance would fit on the head of a pin,' she said.

'Very probably,' he answered drily. 'But you've managed to pick your way past all the disasters you could have fallen into since you left school. Dead-end jobs, rotten relationships and so forth. You have to have a good head on your shoulders to have done that. Also women have an instinct about houses. They see the potential more clearly than men do. On the whole, it's still women who turn a house into a home. They're visualising the furnishings while a man is still wondering if he can handle the mortgage.'

'Presumably a mortgage isn't something you have to worry about.'

'If I needed one, I'd be unlikely to raise it on a property as derelict as this one. My surveyor will probably discover that every known form of rot is rampant and it's thoroughly unsound structurally. But who cares? You've fallen for it. So have I. Between us, we'll restore it to the way it should be, with some discreet modernisations to make it more comfortable than was possible when it was built.'

Holly wasn't sure what he meant by 'between us'.

'Are you putting me in sole charge of the restoration of the garden?' she asked.

'That's the idea…if you're willing to take it on.'

'I'd adore to…but I do wonder if you wouldn't be better advised to get one of the big names in my field to do it. If you were a stranger, of course I'd grab it with both hands and fight off the competition for all I was worth. But you're not…you're a friend, so it's different. Am I the best possible garden designer for this project? I have to ask myself.'

'You're the one I happen to want…and you won't be as expensive as the big shots,' he added, with a teasing gleam.

'You can make your name on this, Holly. You can make Talavera as famous as the gardens at Sissinghurst and Hidcote and Great Dixter. Since I met you I've been doing some homework. I now know a lot more about garden design than I did a few weeks ago. I believe, under your tuition, I could become seriously interested. And perhaps there are things I can teach you.'

There was something in his eyes as he said this that made her breath catch in her throat.

She watched him take a step forward, narrowing the space between them, and she felt like a rabbit hypnotised by the headlamps of a car, unable to move.

Pierce put his hands on her shoulders as he had when he'd kissed her goodbye in his house in London. But this time she knew instinctively that it wasn't going to be an innocuous kiss on the cheek such as people exchanged all the time without altering the nature of their relationship.

Unable to meet the gleaming grey gaze focused on her, she closed her eyes.

When she felt his lips touching hers, her whole body seemed to melt. The pleasure was so intense that it seemed to consume her. She felt like a candle melting into a pool of wax.

By the time he'd stopped kissing her, Pierce had both arms round her. Without their support, she felt she might have fallen over.

Making a big effort to pull herself together, she said, 'I don't think we should be doing this. Business and pleasure don't mix.'

'Not as a general rule—no. But there are exceptions.'

She couldn't believe he could be so in control after reducing her to a quivering bundle of delicious sensations.

'I don't think this is one of them, Pierce. I really don't,' she said, trying to sound firmer than she felt.

She drew away and he let her.

'You're still nervous of me, aren't you?' he said, watching. 'What do you think I'm going to do to you? Make love to you and then walk away, as I did with Chiara?'

Holly felt herself flushing. She said, 'Soon after you'd gone to Africa, Chiara rang up in a rage because I'd told you about the aquamarine. What made you burst in on her like that?'

'It's no use treating Chiara with kid gloves,' he said calmly. 'She's like her mother: self-centred, acquisitive and flighty. She doesn't respond to kindness, which she interprets as weakness. She needs very firm handling. It wouldn't surprise me if your father was too nice a man to keep your stepmother in her place. Women like that can make life hell for their husbands and lovers. I don't think much of Chiara's current meal-ticket. He's a windbag: full of hot air but with no real guts.'

'You're right about that,' said Holly. 'The day after storming at her, he sent her a huge bouquet and offered to take her shopping. But I can't see that your tirade did any good. It hasn't put her off the other man.'

'I went off at half-cock,' he admitted. 'There were reasons for that but I won't go into them now. Let's go back to the car and have lunch. I asked them to put up a picnic. The driver can walk to the pub. It's only half a mile away.'

'I wish I'd brought my camera with me,' said Holly as they left the kitchen garden. 'It's a perfect day for taking snaps. I could have shot several rolls. It's hard to remember everything after only one visit.'

'Once the place is mine, you can come as often as you wish. The pub does B and B and is said to be comfortable. We can make it our field headquarters. If the house were yours, who would you choose to decorate it?'

'If it were mine, I'd do it myself, bit by bit.'

'That would take for ever. Not all professional decorators leave their signature loud and clear on every house they come near. I've heard of a man in Wiltshire who's said to be very good. He advised the Prince of Wales about Highgrove. It's not my ambition to make Talavera a show-place. Let the garden be famous, by all means,' he said, smiling at her, 'but I want to keep the house private. A place for me and my family to escape from the turmoil of the world.'

When he spoke of his family, it gave her a curious pain in the region of her heart.

They had lunch in the sunny hall, beside the open French windows. The driver set up a folding table and two green canvas director's chairs. He spread the table with a green and white gingham cloth.

'We'll do the rest,' said Pierce as the man began to unstrap a large picnic basket. 'You get along to the pub.'

'Very good, sir. What time do you want me back here?'

'Half past two.'

When he had gone Pierce took over the unpacking of the lunch.

'When are you hoping to be able to live here?' Holly asked, standing by.

'Why don't you sit down and relax?' he suggested. 'I should think it will take two years to make the place habitable. Years of neglect can't be repaired in a hurry.'

She watched the deft movements of his fingers as he uncorked a bottle of white wine taken from a cool-bag.

'Was the last owner a direct descendant of the man who built the house?' she asked.

Pierce nodded. 'It's been passed down from father to son for getting on for two centuries. I'd like to think history will repeat itself and my descendants will be living here in the twenty-second century. Continuity is important. I believe in people breaking out of the environment they were born in and having a look at what else the world has to offer. But I also believe in the importance of roots. I had a stable background when I was growing up. I want my sons and daughters to have the same advantage.'

'What if you fall in love with someone who doesn't want to have children?' Holly asked. 'A lot of people are opting out of automatic parenthood these days.'

He gave her a keen look. 'Are you one of them?'

The truthful answer would have been, No, I'm not. I can't think of anything I'd like better than having your babies.

Instead, she said, 'I'm open-minded. I don't think it's a decision one can make in advance. You may be able to plan your future but mine will depend on the man I marry. He might be committed to spending his life in a way which would rule out having children.'

'If he were, would you give up your career for him, just like that?'

'I would rather not, but I might have no option,' she said lightly. 'I think wherever I found myself I could always find something to occupy me, but love isn't something most people get a second shot at. Not what I mean by love anyway.'

'Ah, yes...the man who will make the desert bloom for you.' As he handed her a glass of wine and reminded her of her definition of love, his eyes held a glint of mockery.

'Aren't you having some wine?' she asked.

'I never drink when I'm flying.'

He went on unpacking the lunch, setting out china plates and stainless steel cutlery before starting to open the boxes containing the food.

Holly sipped her wine and wondered if he had any inkling that he was the man who could make the desert bloom for her. Somehow she didn't think so. He had said there were things he could teach her and she didn't doubt it. But what she wanted from him was more than a short course in the delights of physical love.

Remembering his kiss in the garden, she took advantage of his concentration on the lunch to look at the well-cut mouth which had stirred those wild feelings in her. She knew that if it was his intention to seduce her she had little hope of resisting.

She said, 'How did you come to speak Japanese fluently?'

'I enjoy learning languages. Japanese is particularly interesting. You have to adjust your style of speech to suit the person you're addressing and there are words which women use and others which men use. If a foreign man uses a lot of the words associated with women, there'll be jokes about him learning Japanese on the pillow. Which, in case you're wondering, I didn't,' he added drily. 'Fujiko has helped me to master the finer points, but mainly I learnt Japanese on long-haul flights and when there was nothing worth watching on TV.'

After a pause, he added, 'Chiara was a TV addict. Am I right in assuming you're not?'

Holly nodded. 'It was always a bone of contention between my father and stepmother. They didn't have rows about it. He would quietly withdraw to his study. Apart from a few programmes about archaeology and science, he found TV boring.'

'And you?'

'I feel the same way. As a child I watched the box sometimes, but mostly I was busy doing homework. I had to work terribly hard to get the results Dad expected. My stepmother thought him too exacting. But if he hadn't been I wouldn't have done half as well. Not that I was ever at the top of my class. But I did do my best. Children need to be put on their mettle...don't you think?'

'I couldn't agree more,' said Pierce. 'I don't have a lot of patience with any spectator activities. I don't want to watch someone else climbing a mountain. I want to do it myself.'

'Ben says this expedition you and he are doing in February isn't very dangerous. Is that true?'

'Would you mind if it weren't true?'

'Mrs Shintaro would worry if she knew Ben was at risk.'

'Naturally, but would you worry if I were risking my neck?'

She sidestepped the question by saying, 'From what Ben tells me, it sounds as if you often risk your neck...or have in the past.'

Pierce shrugged. 'Perhaps...in the early stages. Not any more. Now my theories have been proved, I have a lot of powerful backing. There would be nothing to gain by having me blown away.'

'When that risk existed, didn't it frighten you?'

'Not as much as getting my project off the ground excited me. Have you been involved in something which involved a degree of risk but an equal or greater degree of excitement and challenge?'

'I don't think so.'

'How about our relationship?'

'I don't see the connection.'

'I think you do,' he said drily. 'But you'd rather not discuss it. When I kissed you just now in the garden, what you felt was a mixture of pleasure and terror. When I asked you if you were afraid of being dumped like Chiara, you dodged the issue. *Is* that what worries you?'

'No, because I'm not going to put myself in a position where you could dump me,' she said levelly. 'Yes, I enjoyed it when you kissed me. But that's as far as it goes, Pierce. I'm not in the market for a casual affair based on sexual attraction. I've been there and done that and it was disappointing. Even you won't tempt me to repeat that mistake. You're very attractive...very charming...but you aren't offering what I want.'

'Which is?'

'An old-fashioned "closed" relationship between two people who don't want anyone but each other...ever.'

Pierce handed her a pair of salad servers. As she helped herself to a mixture of greenery which he had already dressed with vinaigrette, Holly wondered what he was thinking.

But he kept his thoughts to himself, steering the conversation into impersonal channels while they ate the marinated herring which went with the salad.

This was followed by a quiche with a red salad and for pudding there was an almond and honey ice cream from a cooler. Even the coffee, though vacuum-flasked, was unusually good.

'Wonderful food to find in the wilds of Devon,' said Holly.

'Devon isn't as wild as you might think. It's where a lot of downshifters come...people who've had enough of the rat race and want a more civilised life. The woman who put up this picnic is a downshifter. She used to organise lavish buffets and hampers for Glyndebourne and Ascot and the top end of the corporate hospitality market. Then her husband was summarily sacked by a company he'd served well for twenty years and they both decided to downshift. Luckily their children had just finished school. They're twins, a boy and a girl, and bright enough to have gone to university. But they've both decided there are too many graduates competing for too few jobs so they're taking another route.'

Holly was favourably impressed by his intimate knowledge of a family whose fortunes would have had little impact on most of the chief executives whose companies had used the wife's service while she was working in London.

She said, 'It's not only the competition for jobs that's a problem, it's the shortfall between grants and expenses so that by the time students graduate they're in massive debt to their banks. If my father hadn't left me some money, I could never have gone to secretarial college and then on the garden-design course without a bank loan. Being in debt's not a good way to start out.'

'What would you have done without his money?'

'I'd have worked my way through college and done garden design on a part-time, long-term basis. There are courses designed for people who have to do it that way. Which reminds me—the normal procedure at this stage is for us to discuss exactly what you want done here so that I can give you an estimate of how long it's likely to take and what it will cost. And I think, in fairness to both of us, you ought to consult at least two other designers. It's such a prize commission that I'd rather win it on merit than have it handed to me on a plate.'

Pierce drank some coffee, watching her over the rim of the elegant bone china demitasse.

'Is that because you suspect there are strings attached to it?'

'Certainly not! If I thought that, I wouldn't be here.'

He gave her a lazy smile. 'What a puritan front you present, Holly. Repelled by the thought of an overdraft. Repelled by Chiara's use of her only assets, her face and her body. But when I kissed you, you didn't react like a puritan, except for that prim little speech about not mixing business and pleasure. The way your lips felt under mine, and the way you relaxed in my arms while we were kissing wasn't strait-laced. You enjoyed it as much as I did.'

There was nothing she could say which wouldn't be an outright lie.

He read her mind. 'And lies stick in your throat too, don't they? You want to deny it, but you can't. You feel the attraction between us as strongly as I do. But your price is higher than Chiara's. You've just spelt it out for me. Not only marriage but also lifelong fidelity. That's quite a tall order these days.'

Holly tilted her chin, aware that her cheeks were burning, but meeting his gaze head-on.

'It always was a tall order,' she retorted hotly. 'But then so is climbing mountains. If you don't like spectator sports and you're bent on reaching a summit not many people aspire to, why is your love life so second-rate? If your affair with Chiara was anything to go by, your relationships with women are the emotional equivalent of those beds in public gardens where they change the display every season. Personally, I would rather have a single *Worsleya procera* than an acre of showy bedding plants.'

The scorn in her voice made him grin. Angry as she was, it didn't diminish her awareness of the buzz she felt when his lean cheeks formed two deep creases and his lips curled back from those sexy white teeth.

'What's so special about *Worsleya procera*?'

'It's a beautiful blue amaryllis...a type of lily. One bulb costs a hundred pounds and often it takes years to flower. It's a connoisseur's plant...but I don't think where women are concerned you are a connoisseur.' As soon as she'd said it, she realised this wasn't the way to talk to a man who was offering her a commission every garden designer on both sides of the Atlantic would regard as a giant plum.

CHAPTER SIX

'Do you consider yourself the female equivalent of a blue amaryllis?' Pierce asked, his tone sardonic.

Holly's colour deepened. 'Far from it. Chiara might have been that, given different nurturing, but I'm nothing out of the ordinary. What I meant is that—'

Hearing footsteps crunching on gravel, she broke off. The driver had come back early, but he didn't enter the house. She saw him pass the front door, going in the direction of the car.

'I know what you meant,' said Pierce. 'I may not be a connoisseur but I'm quick on the uptake. You're wrong about Chiara, you know. In botanical terms, she's a rose, a climber, the kind with a short flowering season. As for you, except that you're self-supporting, I'm not sure yet what you are.'

Surprisingly, his eyes, which she'd thought would be cold with displeasure at her far too outspoken criticism, were undeservedly friendly.

'My label should tell you what I am,' she said, on a note of contrition. 'I'm afraid I'm sometimes as prickly as my namesake. I don't usually flare up at clients, but sometimes you make it hard to remember that you are a client...or may be a client. If we haven't much time left, I think we should go round again, on a more businesslike basis.'

'There's no rush. As I said on the phone, we can spend the night locally.'

Holly said, 'I left Parson plenty of water, but I don't have any near neighbours to come round and give him his supper and he's probably already eaten all the extra food I left him.'

'In that case, if we can't get back, he'll have to go out and catch himself a mouse or two,' said Pierce. 'Maybe you should have brought him with you. I did warn you about the weather.'

'It doesn't look like closing in at the moment. It's as warm as September.'

'As we came in for lunch, I noticed some cloud building up over to the west. But don't worry. If I can get you back to Norfolk I will…even though a quiet dinner here at the pub would be a nice end to the day.'

For once Holly had no difficulty reading his mind. He was thinking of another agreeable way the day might end. Tuning into his thoughts started a flutter in the pit of her stomach. Why couldn't she be like other women she knew? Although not as brazenly promiscuous as her stepsister, they didn't hesitate to go to bed with men they fancied. They didn't need to be *in* love to make love. It wasn't a big deal to them in the way it was to her.

The fact that she *was* in love with Pierce didn't make it easier. If anything it made it harder. How could she enjoy being in bed with him, knowing that numerous girls had shared the experience before her, and many more would succeed her? If he loved her, it wouldn't matter about his past. That would be something that had happened before she'd known him. Only their shared future would be important.

But not only was it difficult to imagine Pierce falling in love; she found it impossible to see him confining himself to one woman for the rest of his life.

As they were leaving the house, he said, 'Where does a

garden designer start? Explain to me how you begin the making of a garden.'

'It depends what exists already. Sometimes there's not even topsoil, just a battlefield left by the builders. Nowadays the better builders don't lay waste to their sites. If mature trees and shrubs don't interfere with construction, they leave them where they are, knowing they'll help to sell the properties. Some of the big-name developers even have landscaping done before the houses are advertised.'

'Your shoelace has come undone. Stand still. I'll fix it for you.'

With the supple ease which characterised all his movements, Pierce dropped to a crouch and took hold of the ends of the lace.

Looking down at the top of his head, she felt an almost overwhelming desire to reach out and stroke his thick hair. Controlling the impulse took such an effort of will that when he stood up and said, 'Sorry, I interrupted you,' her mind went blank and she couldn't remember what she had been saying.

Perhaps it showed in her face that something had wiped out her train of thought.

He said, 'With one of those battlefield gardens, how would you start?'

'First by talking to the owners...finding out what they wanted—a low-maintenance garden to laze in, or a hobby garden, or a place for their children to play. Ideally, a garden should be an outdoor room, an extension and reflection of the house. So we usually begin with a grid based on the external architecture. It's a very complex process to explain in a few minutes.'

He nodded. 'I realise that. What interests me is that when you start to talk about it your manner changes. Suddenly you're confident and authoritative. But when you're not being professional you're rather reserved and constrained. Or is that only with me?'

'Probably. You are rather an...overwhelming personality.'

Pierce looked amused. 'I wish I could overwhelm you. There's nothing I should like better. But each time I try you close up...like a tender seedling trying to resist being eaten by a large and voracious slug,' he said drily.

Holly couldn't help laughing at the analogy. Without pausing to consider whether it was wise to pursue this line of talk, she said, 'Oh, not a slug...one of those snails with an attractive shell...but just as voracious as a slug.'

'Not voracious at all, actually.' As he said this, his tone was light. But then, his manner changing, he went on in a more serious way. 'You have me filed in the wrong slot. What I was when I knew Chiara is not what I am today. People change, Holly. At that time my working life was unsatisfying and my private life was a reflection of it. For some years I've been ready to try a long-term, stable relationship, but the problem is finding a partner whose life will combine well with mine.'

'Perhaps the solution is for you to become more flexible. It sounds as if you expect all the concessions and adjustments to be made by your partner.'

'As I'm likely to be the primary breadwinner, is that unreasonable? When a woman holds that position, it's logical for her career and her preferred way of life to take precedence. But my work is of real importance in a global context and I shall be doing it for a long time to come, probably past the normal age for retirement. If the woman I marry doesn't take it as seriously as I do, and accept the demands it makes on me, I don't think we have much chance of making a go of it.'

'I'm sure she would respect what you're doing,' Holly

answered. 'But, even if her work weren't as important as yours, it could mean a lot to her.'

'Certainly. I accept that, and I'd want her to keep up her career, making the appropriate adjustments when our children were young and needed a lot of attention. If I were called overseas, she would have to be there for them. You may say it wouldn't be fair for that to be her responsibility, however inconvenient. But the fact is that life isn't fair. Never has been and never will be.'

'I don't disagree with that. Women themselves are coming round to the view that having it all isn't always possible.'

'As the woman who thought up that credo wasn't practising what she preached, it's always surprised me that so many women swallowed the concept for so long,' said Pierce.

Holly had heard the same view expressed by her father and could have rattled off reasons why 'having it all' had seemed an attainable goal to women now in their thirties and forties.

But she felt it would be more productive to return to the point they had started from.

'Oh, look...Miss Willmott's ghost!' she exclaimed, pointing to a clump of *Eryngium giganteum*.

'Why is it called that?' asked Pierce.

'Because Miss Willmott used to scatter the seeds as she walked round other people's gardens. She's been dead a long time...since 1934, I think...but she'll never be forgotten by gardeners who like eryngiums. I'm very fond of them myself. There's a lovely bright blue one which may be around here somewhere. The thing about a garden like this is that you really need to watch and wait for a whole year before you can tell what you've got in it. That's what

I'd recommend you to do, especially if the house is going to take time to renovate.'

'All right, that's what we'll do. We can come down together every two or three weeks and you can make notes and take photographs in the garden while I consult with the specialists about the interior restorations.'

'But you will also consult other garden designers? I'd feel happier if you did.'

'If you insist. Who would you recommend?'

'I'll jot down some names on the way back. You were right about the cloud building up. Ought we to be getting back to the airfield?'

Pierce laid a hand on her shoulder, the one furthest from him. 'If the idea of spending the night here really bothers you, then we'll go back at once.' He looked down at her, cocking an interrogative eyebrow.

'It bothers me, leaving Parson on his own,' she said. 'I know it wouldn't hurt him to miss a meal, but when bedtime comes he'll wonder why I'm not there.'

'What about the nights you spent in London? Who looked after him then?'

'I took him with me in his basket. He likes travelling.'

'I certainly wouldn't want Parson to be frantic with worry,' said Pierce, in a serious tone. And then he threw back his head and gave a shout of laughter.

He knew as well as she did that the reason she wanted to leave had nothing to do with her cat's peace of mind.

That night, tucked up in her own bed, with Parson kneading the quilt and emitting the satisfied purrs of a cat who has yet again proved his prowess as a hunter and is now in domestic mode with a tin of sardines inside him and his housekeeper back from her day out and gently rubbing his chin, Holly felt considerably less satisfied with life than her happy tabby.

From the moment they'd left Talavera, Pierce's manner had been noticeably brisk, as if, having failed to persuade her to stay over with him, he had lost interest.

When they had landed on the Norfolk airfield to which she had driven that morning, she had wondered if he might invite himself back for supper and, later, have another crack at coaxing her to let him supplant Parson as her sleeping partner.

But he hadn't. He had seen her to her car, offered his hand and, without so much as a social peck on the cheek, said goodnight.

Now, mulling over the day, she had a sinking feeling that by insisting he consult other designers she had lost a commission she wanted more passionately than any of her previous heart's desires.

The only thing she longed for more than to restore the garden at Talavera was for Pierce to fall in love with her. That, she knew, was crying for the moon. But the garden could have been hers, and now, more than likely, she had lost it.

The days that followed seemed interminably long as she waited for him to call her. Yet why should he call her? He had talked about visiting Talavera every few weeks, but with Christmas now in the offing he might be otherwise occupied.

For someone like Pierce the festive season would bring many invitations. Probably he would be spending Christmas in some exciting way. Skiing, perhaps. Or flying to a place in the sun to join a house party of important men and alluring women.

For her, Christmas was a lonely time. She had no one

but Parson to spend it with. Once, when Chiara had been
involved with a married man who had gone home to his
family for Christmas, she and her stepsister had spent the
holiday together. But Eric was divorced from his second
wife and would very likely be taking Chiara to the Costa
del Sol.

A week after the trip to Devon, Holly had another visit
from Ben. He took her out to lunch at a country hotel he
had noticed while driving his grandmother.

Holly was surprised and puzzled by this second visit.
Although she liked him very much and thought he felt the
same way, she was almost certain he wasn't attracted to
her. So why had he come? Could Pierce have asked him
to come? But for what possible purpose?

The motive behind Ben's visit emerged during lunch.

He said suddenly, 'Holly, I have a problem I'd like to
discuss with you. I need an outside opinion, but it's not so
easy to find someone whose advice is worth having.
Although we haven't known each other long, I feel I can
trust you to keep my affairs to yourself and to make sensible comments.'

'You can certainly trust my discretion, but I can't claim
to be at all wise, except perhaps a little about gardening.'

'This has nothing to do with gardens,' he said, smiling
at her. 'It's a love problem.'

'In that case why not ask your grandmother…or Pierce?
They both know a lot more about that sort of problem than
I do.' She couldn't resist asking, 'Have you seen him re-
cently?'

'Not for a while. He's a very busy guy. He'll call when
he has a space in his life. There are one or two details to
finalise before we go to Argentina. After that, I must settle
down and get my future organised. The trouble is, I don't

know what I want to do with my life but I do know who I want to share it with.'

He paused, looking out of the window beside their table. Watching him, Holly was struck by the refinement of his face with its subtle combination of East and West. In a *Star Wars* film, he would have been ideal casting for the part of a superior being from a planet where all Earth's problems had been overcome.

As she was thinking this, Ben turned troubled dark eyes on her.

'A year ago I fell in love with an English girl. She feels the same way about me. But because I'm half-Japanese I'm unacceptable to her family.'

'But that's ridiculous,' said Holly. 'Have they met you? Has she taken you home?'

'I've met them several times. On the surface, they were very nice to me. But as soon as they realised we were serious they insisted we stop seeing each other.'

'Why? For what possible reason?' To Holly's way of thinking, any parents who, having met Ben, didn't welcome him as a son-in-law had to be out of their minds.

'It's a complex situation,' he said. 'Charlotte's parents are well-to-do people...or were until a few years back. Then her father was involved in the great Lloyd's disaster. Do you remember that?'

Holly nodded. 'A lot of people were ruined by it. It was front-page news for a long time.'

'Charlotte's parents would have been ruined,' said Ben. 'They lived, and still do, in a large house with lots of land. All their children went to expensive schools. They were only saved from disaster by Charlotte's grandmother. She married a guy with a title and acres of real estate in the centre of London. She's very grand and very rich. She bailed out Charlotte's father and she holds the family purse-strings. The trouble is, she hates the Japanese. If she knew Charlotte wanted to marry one, she'd blow a gasket.'

'Why does she hate the Japanese?'

'In World War Two, her father was a prisoner in Japanese hands. He was treated badly and came back to Europe a wreck. All this time later, his daughter is still breathing vengeance. That the West took a horrible revenge when they dropped atomic bombs on Hiroshima and Nagasaki means nothing to this mean old lady. She's still consumed by a hatred going back fifty years. Until she dies—and she isn't seventy yet—there's no way I can marry Charlotte.'

'Have you discussed this with your grandmother?'

'She thinks painful and unpleasant situations should be avoided. As she can't see any solution, she thinks we should resign ourselves to the impossibility of finding a way through our difficulties.'

'And what does Pierce think? Have you talked to him about it?'

'No, I haven't discussed it with him. I already know what he'd think. He would regard Lady Bletchley as a domestic tyrant. If he were me, he would marry Charlotte without her family's approval. She's twenty. She doesn't need their consent. Knowing Pierce, he would say the financial aspect is her parents' problem. He probably wouldn't be convinced the old lady would cut off the help she's giving them. But what do you think, Holly?'

'I can't go along with your grandmother's point of view. If you're right about what Pierce would think, I disagree with that too. Families are important. If Charlotte loves her parents, naturally she doesn't want to do anything which may cause them hardship. They've been through enough as it is, and the present situation, of being dependent on Lady Bletchley's handouts, must be very difficult for them.'

After a pause for thought, she said, 'Is there any way you could meet her? I'm sure if she spent a little time with you she couldn't fail to like you. She might not revise her ideas about the past, but it could make her realise that people of our generation can't be held responsible for what happened long ago.'

'That's what Charlotte says,' Ben replied. 'You and she are very alike. I'd like you to meet...but I don't see any way I can meet Lady Bletchley. It's obvious to anyone that one of my parents was Japanese. That would be enough to put her off me.'

'She may be grand and rich, but she can't be very intelligent,' said Holly. 'If she'd read any history, she'd know that every nation on earth has committed the most ghastly deeds at some time in its past, and those things are still happening today. She ought to be up in arms about present horrors, not seething about her father's sufferings. How fond is she of Charlotte?'

'She adores her. She's her favourite grandchild.'

'Then how about Charlotte telling her that she's fallen in love with a wonderful American but her parents don't approve of him? She doesn't have to say why and, if Lady Bletchley asks them, they don't have to give the real reason. They could say they don't want Charlotte to go to America where they'll hardly ever see her. Then Lady B will insist on seeing you for herself and maybe...just maybe...you can charm her out of her prejudice.'

Ben gave her a wry grin. 'I think you overrate my charm. She would most probably take one look and have me thrown out. But I guess we could give it a go. In an impasse like this, anything's worth a try.'

When they got back to her cottage, Holly was amazed to see Pierce sitting on the bench outside the front door with an open hamper on one side of him and Parson lying with folded front legs on the other.

'Why didn't you let me know you were coming?' she asked as she opened the wicket-gate.

He rose to his feet. 'I thought I'd surprise you,' he said. 'But I'm the one who's surprised.' He was looking past her at Ben.

Perhaps it was her imagination, but the steely glint in his eyes didn't seem the right expression for a man about to greet a close friend with whom, in a few weeks' time, he was going to share a small tent on a mountain notorious for its capricious weather.

'Hello, Pierce.' Ben came up the path, shook hands and clapped his friend on the shoulder, obviously not receiving the hostile vibrations that Holly thought she had sensed. 'How long have you been here?'

'About an hour and a half.'

'If you'd shown up a little sooner you could have joined us for lunch.' He noticed the hamper. 'Oh, you brought some with you. Too bad I got here first.'

'Don't worry about it. I didn't have to eat alone. I had this guy for company.' Pierce reached down to run his hand along the cat's glossy back. 'But I do have some things I'd like to discuss with Holly in private. As you've had her to yourself since before one, perhaps you wouldn't mind my having her to myself for the rest of the afternoon. A lot of what we have to talk about wouldn't be of interest to you.'

It was pleasantly said but there was no mistaking the firmness underlying the suggestion. Expressed in a courteous way, it was basically an order for Ben to take himself off and the sooner the better.

'Oh…right.' At first taken aback, Ben quickly adjusted his expression. 'I'll be off, then. See you around.'

But as he was turning away Holly grabbed his sleeve. 'Wait…I haven't thanked you for lunch yet.'

'It was my pleasure, Holly.'

After a slight hesitation, he bent to kiss the cheek she offered him.

When he had gone, Holly said, 'That wasn't very friendly.'

'I'm not feeling friendly,' said Pierce. 'How many times has he been here?'

'Only twice. Why?'

'I shouldn't like to see him hurt.'

'I'm not going to hurt him.'

'The only way to be sure of that is to be unavailable next time he wants to date you.'

'Today wasn't a date. It was just a friendly lunch.'

'There's no such thing as a friendly lunch between men and women who find each other attractive.'

'I don't find Ben attractive. I mean, I do in a general way, but not personally…and I'm sure it's the same for him.' She was tempted to add, I *know* it's the same for him, but felt that might lead to questions she couldn't answer without breaking Ben's confidence.

'You may be sure, but I'm not,' was his clipped reply. 'You underestimate yourself. You're very beguiling and Ben is very susceptible.'

'Is he? What makes you think so?'

'Fujiko says he's unhappy. A love affair has gone wrong. He could fall for you on the rebound. He could fall for you, period.'

'I can assure you he won't. We like each other very much, but only as friends. There's no special spark between us.'

'I'm glad to hear it. How about making me some tea?'

'With pleasure.' She unlocked the door. 'I'm sorry your plan fell flat. It's a good day for a picnic.'

The cottage had no hall. The front door opened into the living room which was adequately but simply furnished. Holly had been free to put her own stamp on it with books and other personal possessions from a trunk she had acquired before leaving the house which had once belonged to her father but had later become her stepmother's property.

The kitchen led off the main room. While she was filling the kettle and laying a tray, Pierce wandered about, looking at her books and the paintings hanging in place of the cheap and cheerful prints put up by the owners of the cottage.

'This looks like a Seago. Is it?' he said, looking at a small oil painting of an Arab market.

'Yes, it's the medina in Marrakech. My father bought it...an extravagance he never regretted. I think by now it must be worth many times what he paid for it, but I could never part with it. The painting next to it, of Venice, was my mother's. It's by Glynn Boyd Harte. My parents went to Venice for their honeymoon and she kept a diary in a notebook my father bought her on their first morning there. One day, when I can afford it, I'm going to have a holiday in Venice and go to all the places they went to.'

Pierce had moved on to look at the titles of the paperbacks filling some hanging shelves.

Her memory jogged, Holly clapped a hand to her mouth. 'Oh, hell's bells...I've never thanked you for sending me Daddy's books. I meant to write you a letter and it went clean out of my head. How bad-mannered you must have thought me.'

'We all forget things,' he said easily.

'I bet you never do.'

'I have a PA to remind me.'

'I feel horribly ashamed of myself. It was such a nice gesture on your part.'

He swung to face her. 'Then how about a reciprocal gesture from you...? A kiss would be pleasant.'

He had her cornered, with no gracious way of evading him.

'All right,' she said, outwardly calm, walking towards him. 'But I am very sorry I haven't thanked you before.'

As Pierce didn't bend his head, in order to put her lips to his cheeks she had to rise on her toes and steady herself with her palms on his chest.

'Thank you now,' she said, before kissing him.

He put his hands on her waist, preventing her from backing off. 'A peck on the cheek wasn't what I had in mind. You can do better than that.'

Now he did bend his head, finding her mouth and sending a surge of pleasure through every nerve in her body. She didn't resist him. She couldn't. This was where she wanted to be, held securely in his arms, her mouth parting under his.

It was Pierce who, some time later, put her away from him.

'I think the kettle will have boiled by now.'

Relieved to be let off so lightly, for she knew that already she had lost the power to resist him, she hurried back to the kitchen, hoping her movements didn't betray how dizzy with longing he had made her.

He followed her. 'I'll take the tray. Where do you want me to put it?'

'On the table by the windows, please. I'll open them. We'll still get the sun and the chairs are more comfortable than the bench outside.'

While he was carrying the tray, she found a packet of chocolate digestive biscuits and a plate to put them on. She had never felt less like snacking, but arranging the biscuits in an orderly circle gave her a reason not to join him until she felt more composed. She wasn't used to handling these feelings he had aroused in her.

'I'll pour the tea, shall I? You might spill it,' said Pierce once they had both sat down.

When she flashed a quick glance, he was smiling. He knew the effect his kisses had had on her, damn him.

'I have an apartment in Venice,' he went on. 'We could spend our honeymoon there.'

For some seconds she couldn't believe he had said what she thought he had said.

Reading her mind, Pierce added, 'Yes, that was a proposal of marriage. Not a very romantic one, perhaps, but I can promise you a romantic honeymoon. Venice is the most romantic city in the world...as I expect your mother's diary records.'

'I can't believe you're serious!' Holly exclaimed. 'Why would you want to marry me, of all people?'

Pierce placed a cup of tea in front of her. 'You're the only one, of all people, I have ever wanted to marry.'

'But you're not in love with me...are you?'

'I don't think being in love is the best basis for marriage. Liking makes better sense. I like you very much, Holly. I knew you were the woman I'd been waiting for when you fell in love with Talavera. Falling in love with a house is different from falling in love with a person. A love affair with a house almost always lasts a lifetime. Where's the pot from Talavera you told me about?'

'It's on the large bookcase.' She went to fetch it and give it to him.

Pierce turned it over to look at the words painted on the base. 'Perhaps one day we'll go to Talavera together and choose some more pottery there. You are going to say yes, aren't you?'

'I need time to think about it. You've taken me completely by surprise. I——I thought you only wanted to get me into bed.'

'I do want to do that…very much. I think you want to be there with me. But perhaps it might add to our enjoyment if we postponed that pleasure until our wedding night. Which won't involve waiting very long. When is your birthday?'

'The day before Christmas Eve.'

'Then why don't we get married on your birthday and spend Christmas in Venice?'

'That's less than a month away.'

'So?'

'It's terribly rushed. We've only known each other a short time.'

'But our minds aren't clouded by the usual illusions that cause so much trouble later when they start to fade and reveal all the faults and flaws which were overlooked before. I know you can be prickly. You know I like my own way.'

Holly started sipping the hot tea, hoping it would have a steadying effect. 'I know I couldn't bear being married to a man who was unfaithful to me…even if it wasn't a love match,' she said, in a low voice.

'I shan't be unfaithful. I shall have no reason to stray. On the whole, men don't, if they have all they want at home.'

'I'm not sure that's true,' she said. 'Some men are compulsive gamblers or drinkers and some are womanisers.'

'Any unattached virile man is going to make the most of his opportunities until he finds a wife,' said Pierce. 'We're driven by a powerful urge to perpetuate the species.

The fact that we can control the outcome of our couplings doesn't alter the strength of that driving force. Once we have a woman of our own, the force has a focus. If I give you my word I won't stray, you can trust me to keep it. You trusted me with your life when you flew to Devon in the chopper. Can't you trust my promise that from now on you'll be the only woman in my life?'

'I don't know,' she answered honestly. 'At the moment my head's in such a whirl that I don't know what to think.'

'How long d'you think you will need to recover your equilibrium? A few days? A week?'

'How can I say? It's been such a bolt from the blue.'

'Call me when you've made up your mind. Now I'd better call up the taxi service I used to get here. If I stay, I'll be tempted to use undue persuasion,' he said, his eyes caressing her.

He had made his phone call and was replacing the aerial when Parson joined them, jumping onto the third chair and starting to groom a paw.

'I wonder what he and Louisa will make of each other...assuming you decide to join forces with me?' said Pierce.

'Joining forces makes it sound more like a business merger than a marriage.'

'Marriage is a merger.' Suddenly he reached across the table and captured one of her hands. 'It would be very easy to sweep you off your feet, Holly. But I don't want to do that...not yet. I'd rather reserve that for Venice. In the meantime, I'll only say that, if you do decide to spend the rest of your life with me, I'll do my utmost to make the future a happy one.'

The seriousness of his tone brought a lump to her throat.

How could she refuse what he offered? It might not be the fulfilment of her secret dreams, but it was far more than her rational self had expected.

CHAPTER SEVEN

For two days Holly grappled with conflicting thoughts and emotions. Her head was at war with her heart and she had no one to turn to for wise advice.

Usually, when she had a problem, she would imagine talking it over with her father. Invariably, from among all the things he had said to her while she'd been growing up, there would be something to guide her to the right decision.

But her present dilemma was so far removed from anything she or he could have visualised happening to her that none of her father's codes of behaviour nor anyone else's seemed to cover it.

A marriage of convenience—which was what, basically, Pierce's proposal boiled down to—had been nothing out of the ordinary in past times when women had been dependent on men from the cradle to the grave.

But now, in the closing years of the twentieth century when, even if not in all countries, women had climbed every summit of achievement and no doors remained closed to them, such marriages were an anachronism.

Today, with the exception of gold-diggers like Chiara who would marry for money, women married for love. Which, judging by the divorce statistics, was no greater guarantee of happiness than marrying a man selected for you by your parents, Holly thought, with a sigh as, for the second night in succession, sleep eluded her.

Next morning she overslept, waking with a headache and the insoluble problem still looming over her.

While she was fixing her breakfast, she turned on the radio to hear the weather forecast, forgetting that, as she was up late, she wouldn't catch the programmes she usually heard.

A man with a quiet voice not unlike her father's was giving a talk. For some minutes, with Parson stroking her legs with his furry body and her mind on what she was doing, she listened to the pleasant timbre and good diction rather than to the subject matter.

Then the speaker began to recite some lines she had first heard at Stratford-upon-Avon, at a performance of Shakespeare's *Julius Caesar*.

'"There is a tide in the affairs of men,
Which, taken at the flood, leads on to fortune;
Omitted, all the voyage of their life
Is bound in shallows and in miseries."'

The melodious voice continued but Holly was no longer listening. Suddenly, her mind was made up.

Why hadn't she seen before what now, all at once, seemed obvious? Loving Pierce, she had no choice but to marry him. And perhaps, if she made him happy and helped to realise his dream of how Talavera could be, one day he would find that he loved her.

Wondering if, by this time, he would have left for his office, she tried his private number. After three rings, he answered.

'Sutherland speaking.'

'It's Holly. Am I calling at a bad moment?'

'There are no bad moments as far as you're concerned. How are you?'

'I'm fine. How are you?'

'I'll answer that when you've told me what you've decided. I take it you have decided?'

'Yes. Is your offer still open?'

'Of course.'

'Then I'd like to marry you...I'd like it very much.'

There was silence at the other end of the line.

Wondering if, despite his assurance, when it came to the crunch he might be having second thoughts, she said anxiously, 'Pierce...are you there?'

'I'm here. I'm wishing you were. There are better ways to seal this kind of agreement than by talking. As bad luck would have it, I can't come to you today and I have a raft of appointments tomorrow as well. But I'm free this evening. Could you come and have dinner with me?'

'With pleasure. What time would suit you?'

'Be here by six if you can. We have a lot to talk about.'

'Until six,' she said. 'Goodbye, Pearce.'

'And Holly?' he said, with some urgency, in case she rang off.

'Yes?'

'Thank you.' He had lowered his voice to a more intimate tone. 'If you still have lurking misgivings about your decision, it's the right one, I promise you. We're going to be very happy together.'

'I hope so...for both our sakes.'

'You can be sure of it. Bye now.' It was he who cut the connection.

In case she should need to stay in London more than one night, Holly took Parson with her. As the train was half-empty, she let him out of his basket to sit on the seat beside her, hoping that if a ticket inspector came by he wouldn't insist on the cat being put back inside his travelling container.

From Liverpool Street Station, she took the underground to Marble Arch and from there walked the short distance to an inexpensive bed and breakfast establishment frequented by members of the Women's Institute and similar organisations when they came up from the country to attend their annual conference or have a day's shopping followed by a visit to the theatre.

The reason she hadn't rung Chiara and asked to put up with her was that Holly didn't want to break the news to her stepsister until she had talked to Pierce again and become more used to the idea that by the end of the year she would no longer be Holly Nicholson but Holly Sutherland.

When she arrived at the B and B place, the woman who ran it looked at the furry face peering through the window in the basket and said, 'We can't take pets here, I'm afraid.'

'He won't be here for very long,' said Holly. 'I'm taking him out to dinner with me. He's very quiet and well-behaved. He won't scratch your furniture, I promise you.'

'What about doing his business? Where's he going to do that? Not in one of my bedrooms,' the landlady said severely.

'Of course not. He has a lead. I'll take him for a walk last thing and again first thing in the morning. The thing is, I'd nowhere to leave him and tonight I'm celebrating my engagement,' Holly explained.

The landlady's face softened slightly. 'There's a shed at the back he could sleep in without doing much harm. But not if he's going to start caterwauling and disturbing my other guests.'

'Neutered tom-cats don't caterwaul. Parson might miaow a few times while he settles down, but you see how quiet he's being now. He never made a sound on the tube.'

'Well, all right, I'll make an exception,' the landlady conceded graciously. 'But kindly keep it to yourself. I don't want myself inundated with people's cats, do I?'

Holly arrived at Pierce's front door at five minutes past six. She was tense with excitement, her insides quivering as they had before playing small parts in school theatrical productions and before her college interview.

When Pierce opened the door and saw what she was carrying, he said, 'Is your acceptance conditional on your cat liking my cat?'

'It will be awkward if they don't get on.'

'They'll get on,' he said confidently, taking the basket from her with one hand and cupping her chin with the other.

'Hello again.' He touched her lips lightly with his in a kiss of such unexpected tenderness that it took her breath away.

'It's cold out. Come in and get warm.' He ushered her into the house. 'I debated booking a table at a ritzy restaurant, then decided it would be nicer to eat at home, by the fire. I hope that's all right with you.'

'Anything that suits you is fine with me.'

Pierce laughed. 'I'll remind you of that rash statement in twelve months' time when you may be feeling less compliant. But I'm glad you feel that way now. Let me take your coat.'

He had put Parson's basket down on a hard-seated chair and as he was waiting for Holly to undo her buttons the sound made by a hostile cat drew their eyes to the doorway.

Louisa, who had come to see who was arriving, had noticed the basket and its occupant and was showing every sign of extreme displeasure.

'She may think he's a randy tom who will make unwelcome advances,' said Pierce, ignoring his cat's arched back and indignant face. 'She'll calm down when she finds that he isn't.'

'Perhaps I shouldn't have brought him, but there seemed no alternative,' said Holly, as he took her coat. 'I'm not staying with Chiara this time. I wanted to see you before telling her what's happened.'

'Where are you staying?'

'At a small guest house. If you're serious about getting married on my birthday, I shall need to buy some clothes.'

Pierce hung her coat in a cupboard and then, picking up the basket, put a hand on her waist to steer her towards the studio. There, an elderly man in a black coat and pinstriped trousers was placing a bucket of ice with a bottle in it on the table in front of the sofa facing the blazing fire.

'This is Hooper, who looks after me,' said Pierce.

Holly smiled. 'Good evening.'

The manservant bowed. 'Good evening, miss.'

'Hooper, you are the first to know that Miss Nicholson has agreed to marry me.'

'Allow me to offer my congratulations, sir. I wish you both every happiness.'

'Thank you very much,' said Holly.

'Perhaps your cat would like some water,' he suggested.

'Yes, take him away and give him a chance to compose himself. He was quite rightly shocked by Louisa's display of bad manners in the hall just now,' said Pierce. To Holly he added, 'Don't worry. By the end of the evening they may be sharing her beanbag.' The glint in his eyes added a subtext she pretended to be unaware of.

In spite of what he had said the day he'd proposed this strange engagement, about waiting till they were in Venice to make love to her, he might have changed his mind since then. If he wanted to make love tonight, she had no real grounds for refusing other than an instinctive feeling that it would be wiser to wait.

Although she had some experience, it hadn't amounted to much. If he found her disappointing, he might begin to regret his precipitate proposal. The thought of losing him, before she had had time to learn how to please him, sent a shiver of panic through her.

'Go and sit by the fire if you're still cold,' said Pierce, with a nod at the cushioned club fender. 'Did you walk? Why didn't you take a taxi? Are you short of funds?'

'No, no, I just felt like walking.'

'Well, don't do it again…not in London, not after dark. I don't like the idea of you wandering about on your own, especially encumbered with a cat basket. Women don't have to be wearing a fur and expensive earrings to be targeted by street thieves these days.'

She perched on the fender. She was wearing a straight black skirt with opaque black tights and black leather loafers. Her top was a cream silk shirt, one of Chiara's castoffs.

Holly's pearl studs and single-strand necklace had belonged to her mother. They were cultured pearls, too discreet to make any kind of statement except that of conventional good taste. But none of the ethnic jewellery, bought from market stalls, which she usually wore to go out had seemed right for this occasion. Pierce was accustomed to women who dressed to a high standard of elegance. She didn't want any detail of her appearance to seem cheap to him.

He brought her a glass of champagne. 'To us…to a lifetime of sharing everything life has to offer.'

'To us,' she echoed as they touched glasses.

After tasting the wine, Pierce sat down at the other end of the fender, leaving a space between them.

'As you have no family to speak of and mine is across the Atlantic, I suggest we get married very quietly in my local register office. Or would you prefer a church service?'

'My father was an atheist. We never went to church. I'm happy with a register office.'

'Right, that's the first item settled. What about witnesses? Would you like Chiara to be one?'

'I think she'll be away…in the south of Spain. What about Mrs Shintaro and Ben, as we both know them?'

'No, I think not,' he said. 'I'll ask my two closest friends. There'll be time for you to meet them beforehand. I have a lot of people I want you to meet later on.'

Holly wondered if, despite his friendship with him, Pierce could be jealous of her affection for Ben.

'After we've done the deed,' he went on, 'we'll go to Claridge's for lunch and then fly to Venice. You can buy most of your trousseau there. There are some excellent shops and I'll enjoy helping you choose. Which reminds me…your ring. I had a jeweller whose work I like send round a selection for you to look at. If none of them appeals, they can go back and we'll look for something you do like. I'll fetch them.'

He crossed the room to one of the banks of books, where he touched something, causing a section of shelf to swing forward, revealing a safe. A combination lock opened the thick fireproof door. From the interior Pierce took a shallow box covered with leather. He brought it to the table in front of the sofa and beckoned her to join him. When he opened the lid, Holly saw that the box was lined with black velvet and divided into many small sections, about a dozen of them holding the selection of rings.

'You have beautiful hands. I noticed them the first time we met…I mean the very first time,' he added.

'Really?' said Holly, astonished. She had always taken

care of her hands, wearing barrier creams and gloves to prevent their becoming ingrained with soil like those of many keen gardeners. But she was amazed that he should have noticed them approvingly the night she had thought he disapproved of her.

'Try this one,' said Pierce, taking her left hand and slipping a ring over the third finger. 'No, that's not right. How about this?' He selected another.

'They all look gorgeous to me,' she said, and meant it.

Any one of the rings would have pleased her. They had a distinctive style quite different from conventional engagement rings.

He tried all the rings in the box, fitting them on her finger and studying the effect, unaware that for her it was not the beauty of the jewels which entranced her but the way he was holding her wrist in one hand and trying on the rings with the other. Merely to sit beside him, with one of his long, hard thighs inches away from her lap and his lean fingers circling her wrist was an exquisite pleasure which made her mind boggle at the thought of what she would feel when he made love to her.

'I think this is the right one, but you may not agree,' said Pierce.

'It's lovely. But isn't it frighteningly valuable? What if I lose it or damage it?'

'It will be insured,' he said casually. 'What matters is that you like it. Perhaps you've set your heart on something quite different. If so, you have only to say.'

'I haven't set my heart on anything...except trying to be a good wife,' she said, in a low voice.

His fingers tightened on her wrist. 'Anyone hearing you say that would think you were marrying me for love.'

Holly could not meet his eyes for fear he might see the truth. 'I'm not marrying you for any ulterior motive…unless you count Talavera. But even to have that garden I wouldn't marry just anyone.'

'I'm relieved to hear it,' he said drily. 'Now, to get back to this ring, are you certain you're happy with it?'

'It's beautiful. Thank you, Pierce.'

'Good. That's something else settled. Tomorrow or the day after you can go and confer with the designer about what kind of wedding ring you'd like to go with it. We won't be exchanging rings because I prefer not to wear one. For a climber they can be dangerous.'

He closed the box and took it back to the safe. While he was putting it away, Louisa strolled to the fireside and sat down on the large Persian rug, where she extended one back leg at an angle of forty-five degrees and began some energetic grooming.

Suddenly, pausing, she looked up, fixing large kohl-rimmed eyes on the place, near the back of a chair, where Parson was lurking, looking unwontedly nervous.

Coming back to the sofa, Pierce said, 'Finish what's left in your glass and I'll give you a refill. There's no kick in tepid champagne.'

Obediently Holly drained her glass, her attention on the two cats. 'I think Parson is scared of her.'

'More fool he,' was Pierce's succinct comment. 'It's fatal to let a female of any species feel she can dictate terms. That isn't what they want. It makes them capricious and cruel. If Parson knows what's good for him, he'll come and show her who's boss.'

Holly felt her hackles rising slightly. 'Are you including women in that statement?'

'It's particularly applicable to women. They can't stand a man who dithers. They want him to be in control. If he isn't, they'll give him hell. Your sex is still programmed by nature to need a protective male to stand between them and any threat to their safety. If they find out a man is a wimp, they'll delight in tormenting him. I have an example of that situation among my staff at the moment. An accountant working for us is living with a woman who makes his life miserable. As he's not legally bound to her, it's a wonder he doesn't walk out. But that's part of the problem, of course.'

He stopped speaking, his eyes on Parson who, having retreated behind the chair, now appeared on the other side of it and was investigating the uprights of the fender, pretending to be oblivious to the baleful glare focused on him from the centre of the antique rug.

'That's better,' Pierce said approvingly. 'Pretend you couldn't care less. Louisa's not used to being ignored. Five minutes of the cold shoulder and she'll start making up to you.'

'Let's hope you're right,' said Holly, watching her cat stroll past the fire to sniff the fringe of the rug and then the valance of a slip-covered chair on the other side of the hearth. After satisfying himself that there was nothing hiding beneath it, he jumped onto the chair and gave his shoulder a light lick in the manner of a man who has noticed a speck of something on his immaculate suit.

'D'you mind him sitting there?' asked Holly.

'Hooper doesn't approve of Louisa sitting on chairs, but I don't mind and I don't think this is the moment to undermine Parson's dignity,' said Pierce.

'What did you mean about it being part of the problem...the accountant's problem?' she asked.

He leaned back and crossed his long legs. 'Women have gone along with living together and having children together without any formal commitment. But I'm not sure that, deep down, they're really comfortable with it. I suspect they feel they've lost out. If I had said to you—putting it rather more gracefully—Let's shack up together, what would you have said?'

'Putting it rather more gracefully, Get lost!' she told him, with a flicker of amusement. Then, more seriously she went on, 'My father thought living together was a cop-out…an evasion of responsibility. The irony is that, if he and my stepmother had merely joined forces instead of marrying, when their relationship broke down he could have ended it without, as they say, being taken to the cleaners.'

'If he'd been thirty, or twenty, or ten years younger, he probably wouldn't have married her,' said Pierce. 'The possibility of being taken to the cleaners looms very large in the male mind these days. It's the fundamental reason why, if they can, a lot of men would rather dodge marriage and settle for cohabitation. That doesn't protect them entirely but they usually get off more lightly than a legal spouse.'

'Doesn't the thought of being taken to the cleaners bother you?' she asked.

'It did…until I met you. Then I knew I had found the kind of person who, if, in a place where no one was watching, she found a wallet stuffed with twenty-pound notes but no identification, would go straight to the nearest police station.'

'So would any honest person.'

Pierce crooked a cynical eyebrow. 'People as honest as that are not too thick on the ground, my love. You and I are not going to split, but if we did I don't think you'd run to a lawyer with instructions to take me for every last penny. I think you're the kind of woman who wouldn't even keep that.' He indicated the engagement ring.

Holly was silent, winded by the shock of being called 'my love' in that easy way, as if they were a normal couple to whom endearments came naturally.

Could she bring herself to use loving words to him? Somehow she didn't think so. Not yet anyway.

'It would be nice to think that one day our daughter will inherit it. The pearls I'm wearing tonight belonged to my mother. They're not very special by your standards but they have great sentimental value for me.'

'Understandably,' said Pierce. He reached out to put the tip of his forefinger behind the lobe of her ear and then ran it gently down the side of her neck.

The light caress had an effect as stirring as if he had touched her breast. She sat very still wondering what he might do next, but just at that moment Louisa rose from the rug and walked to the front of the chair where Parson was sitting. As they watched, he folded his forelegs, bringing his face almost to a level with hers. After a moment both cats extended their necks and, with noses almost touching, gave each other a cautious sniff. Then Louisa turned round and, with a flourish of her tail, like a *belle époque* courtesan flirting a large feather fan, strolled away to another part of the room.

'I'm no expert on feline body language, but that looked like the beginning of a mutually tolerant relationship, don't you think?' Pierce asked.

'Yes, I do,' Holly agreed.

Hooper reappeared. 'Shall I serve dinner, sir?'

'By all means.' Pierce drained his glass and stood up. While the butler was lighting the candles on the same table where they had lunched but which tonight was more formally laid with a damask cloth and napkins folded to look like water lilies, Pierce said to him, 'Tomorrow I want Miss Nicholson to choose a wedding ring. I can't go with her myself. You'll be taking the ring box back. Would you pick her up from where she's staying?'

'Certainly, sir. Where is Miss Nicholson staying?'

Pierce looked enquiringly at Holly who gave the butler the address of her B and B place.

While Hooper went away to fetch the first course, Pierce drew out a chair and seated her. 'Let's finish the champagne, shall we? Do you like it, or is it too dry for you?'

'I like it. I've never had this champagne before.' She had noticed the label. 'I can see why it's famous.'

'You'll be drinking a lot of it in future. Now...what else do we need to settle? The rings...the form of the wedding...the lunch party afterwards... Oh, yes, the announcement. How shall we word it? ''The marriage has been arranged and will take place shortly of...'' I'd better write it down.' He felt in an inside pocket of his coat and produced a pen and a diary. 'What was your father's first name, or did he prefer his initials for anything formal?'

'Professor Peter Nicholson.'

As he jotted it down, Pierce said, '*The Times* and *The Telegraph* naturally. What about local papers? The one where you went to school, for instance?'

'That isn't necessary.'

She was beginning to realise what should have been obvious already—that in marrying Pierce she was entering a different world, a milieu involving formalities which had not been a part of her past. Her father, although a don at a major university, had lived in a more modest style than many of his colleagues.

The adjustments she would have to make didn't unnerve her. She was confident she could cope with the public side of their life together. It was merely a matter of studying how things were done.

But the private aspects of their relationship did worry her. Would she be good enough in bed? Would she be able to keep him amused and interested when they were not in bed but were on their own together?

The meal Hooper served was delicious: chestnut soup with the tang of fromage frais in it, a roast pheasant with slices of truffle under the skin of its breast and, to finish, caramelised pears on a bed of juice-soaked sponge cake.

They had coffee in front of the fire while, with almost soundless efficiency, Hooper cleared the table. About half an hour later, while they were listening to music, the butler came back to tell Pierce that he was going home and to ask Holly what time it would be convenient for him to call for her.

After he had gone, she was very conscious that they were alone in the house. By this time Parson had come to sit on her lap, as he usually did in the evening. Louisa, it seemed, was not a lap cat, perhaps because she had been discouraged from settling on her owner's legs.

'If you like you can leave Parson here overnight,' Pierce suggested. 'I should think he'd feel more at home in the conservatory with Louisa, where he can use her litter tray, than in the place where you're staying.'

'They weren't very keen on having him,' Holly admitted. 'Are you sure you don't mind his staying here? I don't think he'll be a nuisance. He's a very adaptable cat and he has met you before, so he'll know I haven't abandoned him.'

'As long as he doesn't expect to sleep on *my* bed,' Pierce said drily. 'It would be a good idea to debar him from yours from now on…get him used to the idea that after we come back from Venice your bedroom will be forbidden territory.'

'What will the weather be like in Venice?'

'It varies. Often it's wet or misty. Sometimes it's very

cold when the wind is blowing straight off the mountains
to the north. Or it can be mild and sunny. Whatever it's
like, it's one of the world's magic places, especially in winter when the Venetians have it more or less to themselves.
I love it whatever it's like. I'm looking forward to showing
you all my favourite corners of it.'

'I'm looking forward to going.' The wine and the food
and the warmth made her stifle a yawn.

'Time you were in bed,' said Pierce. 'I'll run you back.'

He leaned towards her, scooping Parson from her lap and
holding the startled tabby suspended in his strong hands for
a moment before putting him gently on the floor.

Parson gave an offended shudder, adjusting the set of his
fur before looking over his shoulder and fixing Pierce with
an old-fashioned look, so plain in its meaning that Pierce
laughed and said, 'Sorry, old boy, but you might as well
accept you're not the top cat any more. I am.'

Parson's expression had made Holly want to laugh, but
she had suppressed her reaction, not wishing to add to his
sense of indignity.

When he turned round to face her, it looked for a moment as if he might dispute Pierce's authority over him by
jumping back on her lap. But he thought better of it and
stalked off, his tail—held upright when he was pleased with
life—now indicating displeasure by waving from side to
side.

'Don't worry; he's too intelligent not to accept the situation. I like him very much. I'll make it easy for him.'

Pierce put his arm round her shoulders and drew her
against him. With his mouth near her ear, he whispered,
'More than Louisa, as a matter of fact, but I shan't let her
know that.' Then, using his free hand to turn her face towards his, he kissed her.

It felt as deliciously sensuous as a mouthful of chocolate. As her lips opened to his, he used the tip of his tongue to caress the inner edges of her mouth. But there was no thrusting invasion of the kind that had happened before, when she hadn't been ready for it. Nor did she feel his hand fumbling to open her shirt in the peremptory way other hands had. His fingers were touching her throat, exploring the delicate area behind her ear and down the side of her neck.

Suddenly, just when other parts of her body were beginning to tingle responsively, he brought the kiss to an end. Disengaging himself, he stood up. 'I'll go and get your coat.'

He left her surprised and disappointed. She hadn't wanted him to stop and didn't know why he had. There could be two reasons. He had found her response disappointing. Or he was deliberately keeping things under control until he was free to go as far as he liked with her.

But he was free to do that now, if he wanted, she thought, trying to recover her self-possession, not wanting him to come back and find her visibly disorientated.

When Pierce took longer than she expected to bring her coat, she thought it might be because he knew she needed a space to recover, or because he was himself aroused. Men, as she had cause to know, did get aroused very quickly by physical contact with females. Both the previous men in her life had reached boiling point in seconds, making her wonder if she was unnaturally slow.

When Pierce did return, he said, 'I don't want to offend you, Holly, but most brides have parental backing and I know your finances can't be too fluid. In the circumstances, would it affront you if I ordered you the use of my accounts at Simpson and Liberty? They should have something you'd like for your wedding dress. If not, I also have an account at Harvey Nichols.'

'I'm not in the least offended. It's nice of you to suggest it. But I wasn't planning to buy anything wildly expensive. You don't mind if I dress for your wedding at my normal price level, do you?'

'If you buy your dress at a thrift shop, it won't worry me,' he said smiling. 'You seem to be someone who always looks right for the occasion…whether it's a party or a day in the country.'

'Thank you.' She didn't tell him that the only party outfit he had seen her in had been borrowed and must have cost as much as the clothes worn by the women he normally mixed with.

While she was fastening her coat, she said, 'I'll just say goodnight to Parson.'

At first there was no response to the pursed-lip squeaks which usually brought the cat hurrying to see why he had been summoned. Then, at a less eager pace, he appeared round the corner of the sofa.

Holly crouched down to pat him. 'I'm leaving you here tonight. You'll be quite all right and I'll see you tomorrow. Be a good pussy.' She picked him up to give him a hug and a kiss on the top of his head.

He followed them to the garage where, not ungently, Pierce made him stay in the passage while he closed the door. Plaintive miaows could be heard as he opened the passenger door for her. Before entering the car himself, he switched off the garage light. As he got in beside her, he said, 'I expect you feel the same way as mothers whose children go to boarding-schools. I've heard a lot of them say it's an agonising business consigning your darling to the care of other people. Do you think, when I get back to him, a sardine or two might make him feel better about being separated from you?'

'If you have some, it probably would.' To her vexation, her voice came out slightly husky.

Pierce used the gadget which opened the garage door. As it swung slowly upwards and outwards, he switched on the motor.

'Are you going to lie awake, worrying about him?'

'No, of course not. I know he'll be fine. It's just that he was dumped by someone when he was a kitten. I wonder if he remembers that? I wonder if he thinks I'm leaving him?' To her greater chagrin, her eyes filled with tears and she had to look out of the side window in case Pierce should see them.

They were cruising along the street now and a warm hand closed on her thigh and gave it a squeeze. 'Don't cry, darling. Cats aren't like elephants. They don't have long memories. Have you got a hanky on you?'

Darling. To hear him say it, as if she really were his darling, made her want to burst into tears.

'Yes, thank you.' She felt for the tissue she knew was in her coat pocket. 'I'm sorry to be such an idiot. But you see…since my father died…Parson has been like a person to me. I know it's silly to love him as much as I do…but I can't help it.'

The car glided to the kerb. Pierce pulled on the hand-brake and put the gear in neutral.

'Of course you can't help it.' He leaned over to put both arms round her. 'Everyone needs someone to love.'

At that she did burst into tears. 'Oh, dear…it's the wine,' she gasped. 'I don't…make a habit…of this.'

'Don't worry about it. I grew up with sisters. I'm used to tears,' he said calmly, holding her against his shoulder.

His kindness dissolved her completely. The stress she had been through before deciding to marry him, the strain of concealing her love for him, her uncertainty about the future all came welling up to the surface in a burst of uncontrolled weeping.

After perhaps half a minute of letting it all out, with an enormous effort she overcame her emotion and managed to swallow her sobs and bring the outburst to an end.

Drawing away from him, she said shakily, 'Now you'll be wondering what on earth you've let yourself in for.'

'On the contrary, I think the fact that you've managed to let your hair down is a good omen.' In the light from a nearby streetlamp, she could see the flicker of a smile curling the corners of his mouth. 'My father, who's a very wise man—I'm sure you're going to like him—once gave me a kind of summary of what he'd learnt about women from spending the past forty-five years with my mother. One of the things he told me was that if a woman starts crying, whether they're five or eighty-five or any age in between, but especially if it's your wife, the right thing to do is to put your arms round her, not pretend not to notice, or walk away, or get angry. My dad thinks that men should cry more. He says it's a great safety-valve. Are you feeling better now?'

'Much better...and thank you for being so understanding.'

'That's what a husband is for,' he said gently. And then, in a lighter tone, he added, 'I'll be there for Parson too, if he's feeling down when I get back. Come on; you've a heavy day tomorrow. Buying a wedding dress is a big event. Do you prefer shopping alone or would you like someone with you? I suppose all your friends are working.

How about Fujiko? I'm sure she'd be delighted to go with you if you wanted her.'

'I don't mind going on my own. I'd rather be by myself.'

He hadn't suggested the most obvious person to accompany her, she noted. She wondered how Chiara would receive the news of their engagement. She had an ominous feeling that her stepsister wouldn't approve.

CHAPTER EIGHT

'YOU'RE kidding me!' said Chiara, when they met for lunch on the fourth floor at Harvey Nichols.

'I'm serious. I know it's amazing. I can't believe it myself,' Holly admitted.

'I'm gobsmacked,' her stepsister declared.

Inwardly, Holly winced. Perhaps that ugly expression was one that Eric used and Chiara had picked up from him. It might be a good thing if she did take up with the donor of the aquamarine. He might be less coarse and uncouth than her present lover. Chiara had always been influenced by the people she associated with. At school she had fallen in with a group of girls to whom lessons had been a boring interruption to their after-school activities. It was they, to some extent, who had steered her in the direction she had gone.

Deliberately, Holly had kept her woollen gloves on while they'd settled themselves at their table, one of the last few vacant in a restaurant beloved by the store's chic clientele as a rest-stop between bouts of shopping.

Now she took her gloves off, knowing it wouldn't be long before her stepsister spotted the striking ring on her left hand.

As she'd expected, only seconds passed before Chiara gave a smothered shriek. 'Did Pierce give you that? It's gorgeous. My God! That must have set him back a few thousand. Did you choose it, or did he? He always despised things I bought when he wasn't with me. Oops! I guess it's not very tactful to remind you I had him first.'

It struck Holly that there was a perceptible tinge of bitchiness in Chiara's pretended apology.

She said quietly but firmly, 'Pierce is thirty-five and very attractive. It stands to reason that you were one of many. But that's in the past. If you want a place in my future, Chiara, you'll have to stop making gaffes like that outsize brick you just dropped.'

Her stepsister pouted. 'You've become very dictatorial all of a sudden,' she said sulkily. 'If you're going to start being big-headed, I don't know that I want a place in your future, as you put it.'

Holly reached across the table and put her hand over her stepsister's. 'I'm not being big-headed. I'm just telling you straight that although I might excuse your tactlessness I know Pierce won't. I think it would be a great shame if the fact that he had an affair with you years ago meant we couldn't go on being part of each other's lives. You're the only family I've got now.'

After a pause, during which she scowled at the table-cloth, Chiara looked up and said, 'I'm sorry. The fact is, I'm jealous that you've got a wonderful guy who's going to marry you and I'm stuck with a rich layabout who only wants to—'

Holly was fairly well inured to her stepsister's casual use of four-letter words. Fortunately the noise level in the restaurant made it unlikely that two older women lunching at the next table had overheard a word they might have found offensive.

'You're not stuck with him, Chiara. The world is full of men much nicer than Eric. But, if you want one of them to love you, you can't spend the next five years being somebody's popsy. You have to stand on your own feet...make a life for yourself.'

'Doing what?' Chiara said glumly. 'People much brainier than I am are losing their jobs every day. Can you see me working in a shop, living in a bedsit in some dreary suburb, stewing on the tube twice a day? I couldn't take that grind. I'm used to better things. Having lunch here, for example. Let's have a drink.'

When the drinks and their lunch had been ordered, she said, 'I'm pinning my hopes on this guy at Sotogrande. We're going down for Christmas. I'm hoping he'll still be there. I'm not like you, Holly. I don't have a talent for anything. I wasn't tall enough to go in for modelling. I didn't have the right contacts to get into films or television. I'm doing the only thing I can do to have a share of the good life. I know you think I'm a tart, but there aren't too many options for people like me. If guys like Eric are prepared to pick up my bills for half an hour in bed when they feel like it, I think that's better than slogging away as a typist or behind a counter. When are you going to be married?'

'On my birthday.'

Chiara blinked at that. 'Why the mad rush?'

'Pierce sees no point in waiting.'

Holly was tempted to tell her about Talavera, but decided not to. Chiara wouldn't understand the appeal of such a place.

'I hope you know what you're up against,' said her stepsister. 'I'm not trying to put you off. He's a catch...a big one. But living with him won't be easy. He's what they call a control freak...wants everything his way...no argument. I suppose you're madly in love with him. Knowing you, you wouldn't be marrying him if you weren't. I just hope he doesn't hurt you.'

'So far he's been wonderfully kind.'

'Aren't they all, in the early stages?' said Chiara. 'It doesn't last. Hey, I'm going to miss your wedding. I'll be in Spain on your birthday. Where are you going to be married? What are you going to wear?'

Late the same afternoon, Holly found her wedding dress in the Oxford Street branch of a chain which had built its reputation on inexpensive versions of high fashion.

She had trawled all the stores Pierce had mentioned, not with the intention of charging her purchases to his account, but to see what styles women who could afford to shop there were buying at the moment.

The dress she took back to her B and B place in a large carrier was going to need some minor alterations. Better buttons. A hand-sewn hem. The ends of the sleeves turned up an inch. After that, it would take an expert eye to distinguish it from a similar style she had seen on a display model in Harvey Nichols priced at ten times what she had paid for her dress.

A message from Pierce was waiting for her. He would pick her up at half past six and would like her to have her case packed and be ready to leave.

These unexplained orders did seem to support what Chiara had said at lunch about his being a control freak. But after the way he had handled her breakdown last night Holly was prepared to accept that whatever he had in mind had to be in her best interests.

However, it was Hooper, not Pierce, who called for her in a taxi.

'Mr Sutherland would prefer you to stay somewhere more comfortable, with a telephone in your room, Miss Nicholson,' the butler explained. 'He asked me to apologise to you for not being here with you now. He's been held up at his office. By the time you have unpacked and resettled yourself, he will be at your hotel. He's arranged for you to dine there before going to the theatre. He thought you would like to see the new play at Wyndham's.'

'That sounds lovely,' said Holly. 'How has Parson behaved himself, Mr Hooper?'

As he looked to be in his late sixties, she felt it was inappropriate to use only his surname as Pierce did.

'As I told you this morning, when you rang up, he gave every sign of having slept well and his behaviour today has been exemplary. From time to time he has miaowed in a way which I took to indicate that he was thinking about you and wondering when he would see you, but he seems to be a sensible cat, a good influence on Louisa who's inclined to be temperamental.'

'Do you have any pets, Mr Hooper?'

'No, Miss Nicholson. My companions are antiquarian books. My father was a second-hand book dealer so old books are in my blood, so to speak.'

Holly told him about the discovery of some of her father's books in Pierce's library and they chatted companionably until the taxi arrived at their destination, a hotel occupying a row of elegantly-porticoed town houses in a square in the part of London where Pierce lived.

There Hooper handed her over to the care of the hotel staff and very soon she was unpacking in a luxurious bedroom with its own bathroom and a view of the gardens in the square and the early Victorian houses beyond them.

A brochure and tariff inside a leather folder on the dressing table told her the price of the room. It was far beyond her own pocket, but obviously Pierce was going to pay the bill for her. It made her feel slightly uncomfortable to be staying here at his expense before they were married and she wondered what Hooper thought about the arrangement.

She had never known either of her grandfathers and, had they lived, they would have been older than the butler. But she felt he was a cultivated man whose view of the world and its ways would be similar to that of her grandfathers, one a schoolmaster and the other the editor of a weekly newspaper. In Hooper she might find someone to replace those two gaps in her now non-existent family circle.

She spent the day Christmas shopping for Pierce. It was difficult if not impossible to buy a major present for a man who already had everything so she had come up with an alternative she hoped would at least amuse him on Christmas morning.

Wearing the same clothes she had worn the night before, she was ready and waiting in the lobby when he strode through the hotel's entrance.

As she rose from the chair where she had been sitting, he saw her and changed direction.

'Hello, darling. Had a good day?'

Before she could answer, he bent to kiss her on both cheeks in a perfect imitation of a normal fiancé greeting his bride-to-be.

'A lovely day, thank you. How was your day?'

'Tedious. I need a pick-me-up. Let's go to the bar.' He took her elbow and swept her in that direction. 'I'll have a stiff gin and tonic. What would you like?'

As soon as he had ordered their drinks, he turned and gave her a slow, caressing appraisal. 'You have the glow of a woman who's enjoyed an orgy of shopping…second only to that other well-known glow effect. Hopefully, while we're in Venice, you'll radiate even more beautifully.'

The implication made Holly blush, but she found herself thinking that what she would like, instead of dinner, would be to be taken upstairs to her luxurious room and made to glow like that tonight.

'I've arranged for us to have our first course and main course before the theatre and come back for the rest after the play,' he said. 'Now tell me what you've been doing. Where did you go and what did you buy?'

She told him about the film star who had been autographing copies of a probably ghosted autobiography in Hatchards, and seeing a royal duchess buying presents in Harrods toy department.

'What were you doing there?'

'Just having a look. Then I met Chiara for lunch and told her my news.'

'How did she react?'

'With amazement. They're going to Spain for Christmas so she wasn't offended at not being asked to our wedding.'

'I have to tell you that the slob she's with at the moment will never be welcome under any of my roofs,' Pierce said bluntly. 'Of course you're welcome to see her as often as you wish, but as I am never likely to enjoy her company it would be sensible, if you ever want her to stay with you, to have her when I'm abroad.'

'Will you be abroad a lot?'

'Fairly often. Sometimes you can come with me. But in many Third World countries there are health risks I would rather you weren't exposed to, particularly when we decide to have children. I think we should start by having a year or two to ourselves. How do you feel about that?'

'In the circumstances we probably do need more time to get used to each other than an ordinary couple. Anyway Talavera won't be ready for two years. I assume that will be our main home, once it's ready.'

He nodded. 'The pollution level in London makes it no place for babies, if there's a better alternative. I had a country childhood. I'd like the same for my children. Which reminds me—I called my parents today to tell them about us. Later my mother faxed a letter to you.' He felt in an inside pocket and produced an envelope. 'Don't read it now. Keep it for later. If you want to write a reply, the hotel will fax it for you. The number is on the letter.'

'How nice of your mother,' said Holly. 'Wasn't she rather upset at your marrying someone they haven't met?'

'She trusts my judgement. Her main reaction was pleasure that I've finally found a wife. I'm the last of her brood to marry. She was getting worried I was never going to meet Miss Right,' he said, smiling.

His mother wouldn't be pleased if she knew the truth, thought Holly. But clearly he hadn't explained that. Somehow she didn't think he would lie to his parents and wondered what he had said to convince them that she was Miss Right while avoiding saying he was in love with her.

During dinner, at a corner table sufficiently far from its neighbours to make private conversation possible when the staff weren't near, he returned to the subject of children, this time raising the question of which of them should be responsible for the postponement of her first pregnancy.

It wasn't a matter which, at this stage of their relationship, she found easy to discuss.

Seeing her embarrassment, he said, 'You have had a close relationship with a man before, haven't you?'

At her nod, he went on. 'Then I'd guess it was you who made sure no unplanned babies resulted. From what I know of you, I can't see you taking any chances.'

It struck her as a strange remark in view of the fact that, in marrying a man who didn't love her, she was taking a gigantic chance.

She was glad when the discussion ended for, although she knew it was important to talk over everything affecting their future together, in some respects she felt as shy of him as if she had had no experience. His assurance, his air of authority, the deference with which he was treated all combined to remind her that although eleven years was not a huge age gap it gave her a lot to catch up with in terms of sophistication and *savoir-faire*.

'Have you found your dress yet?' he asked, on the way to the theatre.

'Yes, but don't ask me where. I want it to be a surprise.'

'You will have to tell me the colour so that I can order suitable flowers. Or perhaps you'd rather I put you in touch with the florist so that you can discuss it directly.'

The play they saw was a revival of a comedy of upper-class manners first produced in the fifties. The characters' witty repartee and the actresses' glamorous clothes put the audience in a happy mood. But although she enjoyed the performance there were moments when Holly's attention wandered from the stage to the tall man sitting beside her. Although, the night before, she had wept in his arms and been warmed and reassured by his sympathy, he was still very much an enigma to her. She felt it might be years, if ever, before she penetrated the deepest recesses of his nature.

When, back at her hotel, they had concluded their meal, he didn't linger.

'I expect you're missing Parson and I'm sure he's missing you. Come round tomorrow morning and reassure him that you haven't vanished from his life. Come and have breakfast with me.'

They said goodnight in the lobby where, this time, he took her hands and kissed them both in turn.

When she returned to her room, Holly remembered the envelope in her bag. The thick envelope bore the name and address of Pierce's organisation, but the single sheet of thin thermal paper inside carried a New England address.

The letter was typed but began with a handwritten
'Holly—what a pretty name'.

It went on:

I can't tell you how happy we are to hear that our
youngest son has finally found the person he needs to
make his life complete. Of course we are longing to meet
you and hope that will happen very soon after your honeymoon.

Pierce tells me you have lost both parents and have
been on your own for a long time. Soon you will be a
most welcome member of our large family and, from
what my son tells me, a wonderful addition to it. Has he
mentioned my garden and how much pleasure it gives
me? How wonderful to have a daughter-in-law who not
only shares that interest but is a trained garden designer.
I can't believe my luck.

Robert, my husband, joins me in wishing you both as
much joy as we have had since we married forty-five
years ago. We think marriage is still the best recipe for
happiness.

It was signed 'Marianne'.

Holly was touched and encouraged by the warmth the
letter conveyed. That Pierce came from a large close-knit
family seemed a good augury.

She felt she should reply at once and sat down at the
writing table to compose an appropriate answer. After several false starts, she wrote:

Dear Mrs Sutherland,

It was so kind of you to write and welcome me to
your family. Your son is such an exceptional man that I
can't help wondering if I am up to his weight. But I shall
do my very best to be a good wife to him. I, too, hope

that it won't be long before we meet. Thank you again
for your kindness in writing to me. Yours very sincerely,
Holly.

The writing paper provided by the hotel included headed
sheets and blank sheets. She used one of the latter to copy
out the letter in her neatest writing, putting 'Working at'
and her Norfolk address at the top.

By now it was after midnight, but she took the lift down
to the lobby and asked the night porter if the letter could
be faxed immediately, knowing that now, in New England,
it was early evening and her future parents-in-law might be
having a drink before their meal.

'Certainly, madam,' said the porter. 'And your room
number, please?'

Holly went back upstairs, where she used the electric
kettle on the side table to make a cup of hot chocolate and
also ran a warm bath. But they didn't combine to make her
drowsy. She was wound up to a high pitch of excitement,
not only by the unaccustomed taste of London night life
and the realisation of how different her future as Pierce's
wife was going to be, but also by a disturbingly strong
longing not to be lying on her own but to have him with
her, or to be with him in his bed.

An unsatisfied longing for love was something she had
felt before, but never very strongly. Engrossed by her work,
often tired out by hard physical labour, she had never been
obsessed by sex as some of her friends from her college
days seemed to be whenever she was in touch with them.

Perhaps it was partly because she wasn't wound up by
sexy films and the books they laughingly called 'bonkbus-
ters'. She never went to the cinema, hardly ever watched
TV, and mainly read gardening books.

But tonight was different. Several hours in Pierce's company had left her with the feeling that the evening hadn't ended as it should. She had wanted to feel his arms round her, his lips on her mouth, his fingers stroking her neck as they had the night before.

Lying in the darkness of the unfamiliar room with its double-glazed windows and heavy interlined curtains shutting out any traffic noises and her own quickened breathing the only sound she could hear, she wanted more than the controlled caresses he had given her so far.

She found herself longing, urgently, for the night of her birthday when he wouldn't need to restrain himself. What he might do to her then, what feelings he might arouse sent a long, delicious shudder through her. As her body quivered and burned in anticipation, she began to wonder if Pierce might hold the key to the emotional equivalent of a locked room, a part of herself no one else had ever discovered and even she hadn't realised was there.

Next morning Parson greeted her with loud purrs and loving head-butts against her legs as she crouched down to talk to him.

She had picked him up and was cuddling him in her arms when Pierce said, 'If I had rung you last night, an hour after I left you, would I have woken you?'

'No, I was still awake...thinking about the play,' she added untruthfully.

'I was thinking about you...wishing I had stayed with you, or brought you back here.'

She flashed him a startled glance then looked quickly away, unable to meet the fierce light in his eyes.

He came close to where she was standing with the cat in her arms.

'Will you hold me like that?' he asked softly.

Holly's throat seemed to close up. Even if she had known

what to say, the constriction would have prevented her from speaking.

He came closer until Parson was like the filling in a sandwich. Taking her face between his hands, Pierce said commandingly, 'Look at me.'

She obeyed and was instantly mesmerised by the look he bent on her. Once, at the very beginning, she had thought his eyes cold. Now they seemed like windows into a fiery furnace.

'I want you,' he said, in a low voice. 'I've wanted you from the moment I called you a prig and you damn nearly lashed out and hit me. But I'll wait till we get to Venice, till you're my wife. I don't like to run with the herd. I like to do things my own way.' Softly, he traced the line of her cheekbones with his thumbs. 'We're probably going to be the first and last couple in years who haven't been to bed before the wedding. But it'll be worth the waiting. You're going to remember your wedding night for the rest of your life…I promise you that.'

It was Parson, beginning to wriggle, who brought an end to the moments of motionless silence which followed that husky-voiced pledge. Pierce removed his hands from her face and stepped back to allow the cat to drop lightly to the floor.

At the same time Hooper appeared with a tray of break-fast things.

After Pierce had indicated that she should follow the butler, Holly said, 'I think I'll go back to Norfolk this afternoon. I've got a few more things to buy…tights to go with my dress and so on…but I am still a working woman and can't take too much time off if I'm taking a long break at Christmas.'

The butler was on his way to a large, light conservatory. While he was transferring the things on the tray to a breakfast table already spread with a crisp cotton cloth, Pierce asked her, 'With a project like the one you're working on now, how are you paid? In instalments?'

'Yes. The clients wanted me to oversee the job from start to finish but obviously, during the winter, there are periods when the weather holds up progress. I worked out what it would cost me to live locally and added what I felt was a reasonable fee for the time I was likely to be actively involved. They accepted the total and we arranged to split it into three instalments. They're out of the country themselves at the moment. As soon as they're back, I'll explain what's happened. I'm sure they'll be very understanding and it shouldn't make a lot of difference.'

After being dropped by Pierce in Bond Street, Holly spent the morning buying underwear for Venice. She didn't waste money on an expensive nightdress which she knew she wouldn't be wearing, but she did buy herself a new dressing gown: not a frilly feminine number, which she didn't think Pierce would like, but a plainly styled robe of silky-looking striped rayon, the predominant colours violet and deep dark red.

After a sandwich lunch, she went back to the hotel, from which she had checked out earlier, to collect her case from the baggage room. Then she took a taxi to Pierce's house to put Parson in his basket and say goodbye, for the time being, to Hooper and Louisa.

On the afternoon before her wedding, she returned to the same hotel in time to bath and change for a dinner party given by Mrs Shintaro. Ben was going to be there and Holly was curious to know what was happening to his love life. He hadn't called her since the day they had lunched together and Pierce had been markedly cool towards him.

In the interval since her last visit to London, Pierce had called her every day, but his manner had been matter-of-fact. He had never repeated the things he had said to her on the last morning at his house, or made any similar remarks.

When he arrived to take her to Fujiko's apartment, she was wearing an outfit she had happened to see in the window of a country dress shop after mailing her Christmas cards from the nearby post office.

It was a colour she never normally wore—the bright red of holly berries. But at this time of year it seemed appropriately festive. Surprisingly cleverly cut for the price, it clung to her figure in a way that contradicted the long sleeves, the conservative length of the skirt and the modest depth of the V-neck.

When, having stayed in her room until notified of Pierce's arrival, she stepped out of the lift and walked to where he was waiting, he didn't come to meet her. She could see that he was surprised, but whether favourably or unfavourably she couldn't be sure.

Her wrap, a black lambswool shawl with a braided edge, was folded over her arm. In her other hand she had a small black purse with, inside it, the slip of plastic which unlocked the door of her room.

'Hello,' she said, smiling, lifting her cheek for his kiss.

'Hello.'

As he bent towards her, she caught an elusive whiff of some fresh-smelling aftershave. He always looked and smelt cleaner than other people. She had never seen him with hair that didn't look recently washed. His nails always looked as immaculately scrubbed as a surgeon's.

'I've never seen you in red before. That's a terrific dress.' He was looking at the way it was moulded to her breasts and hips.

'Thank you.' She shook out her wrap. 'It was mild when I arrived but perhaps it's colder out now.'

He had come in a taxi, no doubt in order to drink more freely than he would if driving. Outside the hotel, the same taxi was waiting to take them on to the party. As she stepped in and settled herself in the far corner, Holly wondered if, on the way there, he would kiss her again.

The interval since their last meeting had seemed far longer than it had actually been. He had stirred something in her which now wouldn't leave her in peace. She had thought of little else but their honeymoon and his promise to make their wedding night unforgettable. Now their arrival in Venice was less than twenty-four hours away.

'Did you drop Parson at the house? I haven't been back since this morning. I knew I'd be running late so I took a change of clothes to the office and had a shower there,' he said as the taxi moved off.

'Mr Hooper told me you had a lot on today. Are you bushed? Is a party the last thing you want?'

'The sight of you in that red dress revitalised me. I just wish this trouble in Africa hadn't blown up right now. There's been enough strife there already without a fresh outbreak.'

Holly had seen a newscast on the TV in her room. But, preoccupied by this important juncture in her own life, she hadn't paid much attention or realised that trouble in one of the African countries might affect his organisation.

'We could postpone our trip if you feel you ought to stay here,' she said.

'Are you kidding? Postpone my honeymoon? Not damn likely.'

He moved to the centre of the seat to take possession of one of her hands and hold it in his on his thigh.

His fingers were warm and, close to him, she could sense

the strength of his vitality almost as tangibly as the heat from a radiator. It took more than a long, busy day to diminish his driving force.

'This time tomorrow we shall be in my place in Venice,' he said, lowering his voice, although the glass partition behind the driver was closed and he couldn't hear them. 'You'll be the first person to stay there. It's a part of my life I've never wanted to share before.'

Somehow this made her feel such a strong rush of love for him that she couldn't control the impulse to snuggle against him, bending her cheek to rest on his shoulder for a moment as she said, 'I'm longing to be there.'

'Do you mean that, Holly?'

The sudden tightening of his fingers made her suppress a gasp.

'Of course I mean it. I—' She bit back the words on her tongue. Straightening, she said, 'I've learnt a few words of Italian. Just "please" and "thank you" and so on. I suppose you speak Italian fluently?'

'Yes.' His tone was abrupt.

Sensing his displeasure, Holly wondered if her instinctive gesture was not what he wanted from her. Perhaps it had been too childlike, or too much like Parson's displays of affection. Perhaps what Pierce wanted from a woman wasn't that kind of gesture but only signals of desire. Perhaps he was holding her hand on his thigh in the hope that she would caress him in a more exciting, inviting way.

But he must know she wouldn't do that...couldn't do that...not yet. They were not on those terms. She could imagine if he loved her, casting inhibitions to the winds and becoming as wanton as he wished. But a one-sided love was not the right climate for total abandonment, except, perhaps, when the lights were turned out in their bedroom.

It wasn't far from her hotel to Fujiko Shintaro's apartment. On arrival, a liveried doorman came forward to open the door and Pierce sprang out and turned to help her alight. While he paid the fare, Holly rearranged her wrap.

'Not so cold tonight, miss,' said the doorman. He was young and his smile was admiring.

Holly smiled back, as she did at everyone who was pleasant. 'It doesn't look as if there's going to be a white Christmas after all.'

'There's snow in the north.' The doorman's eyes were saying that he fancied her.

At that moment Pierce turned round, intercepted the look and gave the young man an arctic stare which made him redden and look down.

To Holly's astonishment, when they entered the lobby where an older member of the apartment block's staff was on duty, he said, 'Your doorman needs some more training in keeping his thoughts to himself. He'll explain what I'm talking about. Have a word with him, will you?'

'Yes, sir. Certainly, sir.' If the man was baffled, he didn't show it but ushered them into the lift.

On the way up to the penthouse, Holly said, 'Wasn't that rather severe, Pierce? You could get the doorman into trouble.'

'He's asking for trouble, looking at women like that. He's lucky I didn't swat him.' Pierce sounded and looked tense with anger.

As the doors of the lift slid apart, Holly felt a frisson of apprehension. Long ago, in one of his talks about life and how to live it, her father had warned her about jealousy.

She could still remember his words. 'Jealousy is a sickness...a mental illness. People who suffer from it see the world through a distorting lens. They suffer terribly themselves and they make other people's lives hell. No matter how much you like someone, if you see signs of jealousy, steer clear of them, Holly. They're dangerous people to mix with.'

As she removed her wrap, she looked up at the face of the man she was going to marry at half past eleven tomorrow and saw little knots of sinew at the angles of his jaw and a stormy look still in his eyes.

Was this the first intimation that Pierce was one of the people her father had warned her about?

CHAPTER NINE

IT WAS a party for twelve and almost everyone present had, like Pierce and herself, been born in a different country, even the married couples being a combination of nationalities. Only the hostess and her grandson had visible links with the same culture. When they went into dinner, Holly found herself next to a Frenchman many years older than herself.

'You are the beautiful garden designer who has swept Pierce Sutherland off his feet, so Fujiko tells me,' was his opening gambit.

'I wouldn't say that, but we are engaged to be married,' Holly said, smiling.

'You are too modest, *mademoiselle*. Were I thirty years younger, I should also be at your feet.'

He flirted with her all the way through the first course. But when Holly glanced down the table to where Pierce was sitting, wondering if he was aware of the Frenchman's light-hearted attentions and was taking them seriously, he caught her eye and gave her a friendly wink.

Perhaps he had the sense to see that although her neighbour was playing the part of the gallant Frenchman for all he was worth, it was only in fun, and he had a very attractive Irish wife with whom, from time to time, he exchanged affectionate glances.

With the arrival of the second course, they both turned to their other neighbours, Holly's being a Swede in his forties. From him she learnt that in the far north of Norway, because of the long hours of daylight and the effect of the Gulf Stream, rice could be grown. She filed this away to tell Pierce, hoping it would interest him, if it wasn't something he already knew.

It wasn't until after dinner that she had a chance to talk to Ben, although only in the company of other people, so that she couldn't ask what she wanted to know.

Presently, he said to the others in the group. 'Would you excuse us? There's a Japanese painting Holly wants to see. It's in another room.'

On the way there, he said, 'As you probably guessed, I want to talk to you privately. We'll go to my grandfather's study. We shan't be disturbed there.'

'I wasn't sure you would be here tonight,' said Holly. 'I thought you might have gone back to America.'

'I've been in the north of Scotland, trying out the tent Pierce and I will be using on Aconcagua.' He opened a door, feeling for the light switch before standing aside for her to precede him into a room lined with books and furnished with a large desk and two comfortable chairs on either side of a library table.

'When he died, my grandfather was writing the second volume of his definitive work on the artists who specialised in carving netsuke,' said Ben. 'Do you know what they are? Come over here and I'll show you some.'

He gestured towards a glass-fronted alcove between the rows of massed books. When he touched another switch, the alcove illuminated, the better to show a display of small carvings in ivory and wood.

'Netsuke—it's spelt N-E-T-S-U-K-E but pronounced *netski*—the toggles are used to anchor medicine boxes and purses to traditional Japanese costume,' he explained.

They're an important art form. If you want to see a very fine collection of them, go to the Victoria and Albert museum.'

After giving her a minute or two to admire the carvings, many in the form of rats, mice and other small animals, he said, 'I want to thank you for the advice you gave me when I came to see you in the country. We did as you suggested and it worked. It turns out that Charlotte's grandmother is no longer as violently anti the Japanese as she used to be. Do you remember the VJ celebrations in the summer of 1995?'

'Of course,' said Holly, who had seen on television the parades and other functions commemorating the end of World War II in the Far East.

'It seems the old lady saw a programme on TV which made her realise how much the Japanese had suffered. Charlotte's parents hadn't grasped that her attitude has changed. It's a subject they've always avoided discussing with her so they didn't know her outlook has mellowed.'

'That's wonderful, Ben. I'm so glad for you. Does that mean that you and Charlotte will be emulating us pretty soon?'

'I hope so. I may even return to my father's law firm. I never wanted to before, but now it seems more attractive. Anyway, I'm grateful to you, and I hope, soon after you come back from your honeymoon, I can get you together with Charlotte. She's very keen to meet you. This is from both of us.'

He put his arms round her and hugged her.

It was a spontaneous gesture to which Holly responded with real affection, hoping that the young American and the girl he loved would become lasting friends.

As they drew apart, smiling warmly at each other, a voice from the doorway said, 'Is this a private party, or can anyone join in?'

Holly was startled into an audible gasp. Ben had steadier nerves. Without any visible surprise, he said, 'Come on in. I've been showing Holly some of the netsukes. Is the party starting to break up?'

Pierce said coldly, 'Not that I've noticed, but it's time she and I left. Holly has a big day tomorrow.'

'At least you aren't having a huge wedding with all the strains that involves,' Ben said, smiling at her, apparently unaware that his friend's tone had not been friendly. 'I hope when I tie the knot I can persuade my bride to do it quietly and privately. Aside from the massive cost of a fashionable wedding, who really enjoys that kind of three-ring circus?'

Neither Pierce nor Holly made any comment on this. They all left the room, Ben switching out the lights and closing the door behind them.

When Holly said goodnight to their hostess, inwardly she felt a good deal of embarrassment because Mrs Shintaro had not been invited to the wedding or the lunch at Claridges afterwards.

Whatever Fujiko felt inwardly about being excluded, there was nothing but warm affection in her manner during their parting exchange.

Going down in the lift, Holly said nothing, waiting for Pierce to break the silence. But he didn't speak.

A different doorman from the one who had annoyed him earlier was on duty now and within moments of their leaving the building a taxi had seen this doorman's signal.

Stepping into it, Holly knew that even if Pierce chose to ignore the incident upstairs she couldn't let it pass.

For several minutes after the taxi had set off, she waited for him to initiate the kind of discussion about the party people normally had after going out together. But the minutes passed and he said nothing, staring out of the windows on his side of the vehicle with his face turned away at an angle which emphasised the slant of his cheekbone and the clean, taut line of his jaw.

At last she could bear no longer the unspoken tension between them.

She said, in a quiet, even voice, 'Are you going to make a habit of following me every time I disappear with another man...even one who's a close friend of yours?'

For some seconds she thought he was going to ignore the question. That irked her even more. Sulking drove her to distraction. She had thought it a hateful weapon since seeing her stepmother use it against her father.

But then Pierce spoke. 'I wasn't aware that you had disappeared until I looked round and you weren't there. I assumed you had gone to the bathroom, but you were away so long that I began to wonder if you weren't feeling well. When I spoke to Fujiko, she said you had left the room with Ben. Not very civil behaviour by anyone's standards.'

'That's ridiculous,' Holly said crisply. 'Ben had something to tell me that wasn't for public consumption. If I'd seen you leave the room with Fujiko, I would have thought nothing of it.'

'Fujiko is older than my mother. Ben isn't an elderly man. He's not much older than you are.'

She could no longer repress her mounting indignation. 'He's your *friend*. He's been testing the tent you're going to share on Aconcagua. Can't you trust him to spend ten minutes alone with your fiancée? Can't you trust me?'

'You misunderstand my concern,' he said coldly. 'I warned you before that you underestimate yourself. The way you look tonight, every man there was admiring you. You should be aware of your power and use it more circumspectly.'

Holly decided that, even though Ben hadn't told Pierce

his news yet, if he knew the trouble it was causing he wouldn't object to her being the one to tell it.

She said, 'I could be the most alluring woman in the world. It wouldn't have the smallest effect on Ben. He's still in love with someone else and it's going right for them now. That's what he wanted to tell me. That's why he was giving me a hug. Because he's relieved and happy and he thinks I helped him get over his problem.'

'How did you help?' Pierce asked.

'It's a long and complicated story. I'll tell you some other time. At the moment I'm too upset by the way you've behaved. You went over the top about the doorman and you were obviously furious when you saw Ben and me exchanging a perfectly innocent hug. If that's how you're going to be for the rest of our lives, I have to ask myself if I can live with a man who starts being suspicious and angry with so little reason.'

He shot out a hand, grasping her by the wrist, his fingers painfully tight. 'I don't like it when other men leer at you in my presence. He was out of line and deserved a sharp reprimand.'

'Ben didn't deserve to be glared at. It's the second time you've been foul to him for no reason…and you're hurting my wrist.'

'I'm sorry.' His fingers slackened, but he didn't let go.

In the half-light of the taxi, its interior intermittently brightened by the beams from streetlamps and shop windows, they stared each other down.

Although in her heart she felt a sick despair that all her bright dreams of making him love her seemed about to blow up in her face, Holly refused to be routed by the fierce gleam in his eyes.

If she didn't stand her ground now, she was giving him

tacit permission to ride rough-shod over the rest of her life…if, after this, they could make a life together.

'I don't think Ben noticed,' he said. 'He's not as sensitive as you are.'

'Then you admit you were jealous?'

'Yes, for a moment, I was. Is that a crime? Would you rather I had been indifferent?'

At this point the taxi pulled up outside the hotel, where a couple in evening dress were waiting for transport. Even if they hadn't been there, waiting for Pierce and her to vacate the taxi, Holly wouldn't have been able to reply immediately. She needed time to think how best to answer.

The doorman opened the door and she stepped out first, moving out of the way while Pierce paid the fare and the other couple got in. He must have given the driver a twenty-pound note and the man was short of change and took a little time to find the necessary money.

Holly looked at Pierce's broad shoulders and remembered the night she had leaned against him and wept. She wished she understood him. Was it madness to marry a man she couldn't rely on to behave in a way she found acceptable? Was the brutal pressure of his fingers on her wrist the first intimation that, given what he considered sufficient provocation, he might even be physically cruel to her? Or was that horrible possibility a figment of her imagination, prompted by an article on domestic violence in the paper she had read on the train this morning, plus a bad case of pre-wedding jitters?

She heard him say goodnight to the driver and then he turned towards her, his expression inscrutable.

'We have to talk this out. I'll come in with you.' Inside the lobby, he said, 'Would you like some coffee?'

'Why not?' said Holly. 'It's not going to keep me awake. I'm unlikely to sleep much anyway.'

Pierce ignored the rider, turning towards a quiet corner of the large entrance lounge, having first made a sign to the night porter that he would require service.

Within moments of their sitting down in two armchairs arranged at right angles to each other, a waiter appeared. 'Yes, sir?'

'A pot of coffee and two glasses of Remy Martin brandy, please.'

'Certainly, sir.'

'Now,' said Pierce, when the man had gone, 'let me repeat my question. Would you prefer me to ignore other men's attentions to you?'

'You didn't go overboard when the Frenchman I was sitting next to at dinner was flirting with me.'

'I know him. He behaves like that with every attractive female. It doesn't mean anything.'

'You should have known that Ben hugging me was equally harmless.'

'Did I suggest that it wasn't?'

'You didn't say so…but you looked angry. Your whole manner was hostile.'

He was sitting with his elbows on the arms of the chair and his hands loosely clasped. Now he unclasped them, placing his closed fingers on either side of his nose and closing his eyes for a moment.

The gesture reminded her that he had already had a difficult day because of the crisis which had blown up in Africa. In spite of her own hostile feelings, suddenly she found herself wanting to put her arms round him and hold him the way he had held her when she had been overwrought.

Instead, she said, 'Perhaps, as I suggested earlier, we should put off the wedding for a bit. You have other things on your mind now. It's not as if a postponement would upset a mass of elaborate arrangements and disappoint scores of guests.'

He opened his eyes and dropped his hands. 'Is that what you want to do?'

'I want what's best for both of us. Maybe we've rushed into this. Maybe we need more time.'

'You may,' he said. 'I don't. I never go back on decisions. I only make them when I'm sure that what I'm planning is right.'

The waiter came back. They watched in silence while he arranged a coffee-pot, sugar, cream, cups and saucers, two balloon glasses of brandy and a dish of chocolates.

'Are you staying here, sir?'

'No, but Miss Nicholson is. It can go on her account,' said Pierce, handing him a tip.

'Thank you very much, sir.' The waiter offered her a pen to sign the bill.

After she had poured out the coffee, she said, 'I wish I had your confidence. It's such a momentous step…marriage. People hope they've made the right choice but only time proves them right.'

Pierce drank some coffee and chased it down with almost the whole glass of brandy.

'You'd better sleep on it, Holly. I can't make up your mind for you. Perhaps your subconscious will. I'll say goodnight.'

He crossed the lounge and, without turning round when he reached the door, left the hotel.

On the day of her wedding—if it were going to take place—Holly was woken at nine by her alarm clock. In the early hours of the morning she had re-set it so when eventually she did fall asleep she wouldn't be woken up early.

First she had a shower and then, knowing it was served

until ten, she ordered a continental breakfast. That done, she dialled Pierce's number.

The call was answered by Hooper. 'Mr Sutherland's residence.'

She was too strung up to stand on ceremony. She said, 'This is Holly. May I speak to Pierce, please?'

'He isn't here, Miss Nicholson. He's in the park, on his roller-blades.'

'His roller-blades?' she echoed, astonished.

'Mr Sutherland has been roller-blading since the sport started in this country. He's extremely expert. He says it concentrates the mind. Did you just want to speak to him, or has some kind of hitch arisen? If so, perhaps I can help?'

'There's no hitch. But I do need to talk to him. Does he have a cellphone on him? Can you make contact?'

'Unfortunately not. He prefers to be undisturbed. But I'll ask him to call you the moment he returns.'

'Thank you. Before he went out...did he seem his usual self, Mr Hooper?'

'I would say so, yes.' After a slight pause, he added, 'Are you feeling nervous this morning?'

'Yes,' she admitted. 'I'm wishing my father were here to calm me down.'

'Perhaps, if you wouldn't think it impertinent, I can offer some reassurance.'

'Please do, if you can.'

'A long time ago I was married myself,' he said. 'Unfortunately we had no children and my wife died young...in her forties. But until then we were very happy...and I'm sure you and Mr Sutherland are equally well suited. It's very natural to feel nervous in the last hours before your wedding. In a few days' time, when you're together in Venice, you'll look back and smile at this morning's feeling of stage fright. Naturally, Mr Sutherland doesn't discuss personal matters with me, but I know him well enough to be sure that he's been a much happier man since he met you, Miss Nicholson. If that also holds true for you, as I'm sure it does, can there be any doubt that much happiness lies ahead of you?'

'Thank you, Mr Hooper...thank you.' She was too moved to say more.

It was half an hour later, and she had finished her breakfast, when the telephone rang.

'Hello?'

'It's Pierce. You wanted to speak to me.'

'Only to say good morning...and that it seems a long time till half past eleven.'

'You're going to be there, then?'

'Yes, I'm going to be there.'

'Good. I was hoping you would be. How did you sleep?'

'Not very well. And you?'

'Hardly at all. But tonight, with you in my arms, I'll sleep a lot better. Until half past eleven...'

Holly left for the register office escorted by Pierce's friend, whom she had met before. He made all the right remarks about her outfit—a simple cream dress and a cap of Christmas roses with clusters of golden stamens among white silk petals. From then on the day, after starting slowly, suddenly switched to fast forward.

The short wedding ceremony, the lunch with the witnesses, the drive to the airport, the unaccustomed luxury of the first-class lounge, the short flight to Italy, the final lap of the journey in a fast launch from the airport across the lagoon all seemed to follow in rapid, dream-like succession. None of it felt like real life, except that, when she looked at her left hand, there beside her lovely engagement ring was the plain gold ring symbolising her new identity as a married woman. All that remained was for Pierce to make her his wife in the fullest sense—an act which most bridegrooms performed a long time before the wedding but he, for reasons of his own, had chosen to delay.

Italian time being an hour ahead of London time, it was dark before they reached Venice, which was first seen as a shimmer of lights which seemed to rise from the sea like those of some magical city in a fairy tale.

The runways at Gatwick had been wet from a steady drizzle, but here it was a dry, clear evening and not too cold to stand outside the cabin and breathe in the salty air and watch the city take shape.

Pierce put his arm round her shoulders, drawing her close to him. It seemed to her that she could feel the warmth and vigour of his body even through their thick winter coats.

'By this time tomorrow,' he said, 'I hope you'll feel the same way I do about this extraordinary place. From the first time I saw it, I loved it. But perhaps if I lived here the magic would dissipate. It's better to come and go and never to stay too long.'

The launch slackened speed to enter a canal just wide enough to allow two-way water traffic. Tall houses loomed on either side, the lights from their windows reflected in the water.

'A lot of Venetian apartments, especially the ones on the upper floors of the old *palazzi*, have very low ceilings,' said Pierce. 'For somebody tall that's not comfortable, so I bought a place with more headroom. I hope you're going to like it.'

'I'm sure I shall love it. Oh, Pierce!' Her exclamation was caused by the launch gliding under a bridge and leaving the canal behind as it swung to the right and presented her with a view she had seen many times in paintings of

Venice but which held her spellbound as she took in the busy waterfront and what she knew had to be the mouth of the Grand Canal itself.

They went in a different direction, passing a point of land and cruising along another waterfront on one side of a wider channel.

'You can get your bearings tomorrow,' said Pierce. 'This evening the names don't matter. You must be tired. It's been an exhausting day for you.'

'I can think of a lot of people who wouldn't mind being exhausted in such nice ways,' she said, smiling. 'Who looks after your place for you?'

'A maid comes in every morning when I'm here and twice a week when I'm not, to keep an eye on things. Apart from breakfast, I eat out. Tonight we'll stay home and picnic, if that's OK with you. My secretary called Lucia and gave her a list of stuff to leave in the kitchen for us.'

His place was part of a building which had its own watergate. The launch drew alongside the mossy step and the boatman made fast while Pierce helped her to step out, leaving the boatman's assistant to deal with their luggage.

'Alone at last,' Pierce said, smiling, when the cases had been brought up, the bringer of them tipped and the outer door closed behind him. 'Come on, I'll show you round and then you can either unpack or lie in a hot bath while I make a cup of tea or fix you a drink. Whatever you want, you shall have, *bella signora.*'

The main room, where they were standing, was so full of interesting things that she couldn't take them all in, but only formed an impression of treasure trove from his travels or perhaps found here in the city, like the eye-catching bust of a Moor with a black marble face and rose marble turban and tunic.

'The bedroom is through here.' He led her along a corridor, lined with books and lit, in the daytime, by a window of small leaded panes the size of saucers, to the most romantic bedroom Holly had ever seen or imagined.

Its side walls were lined with panels of antique mercury glass. Behind the bed was an enormous landscape, painted on unstretched linen, of islands in a blue sea. The bed itself had four posts, each about four feet tall and topped with a gilded swan spreading its wings.

'What a wonderful bed! Is it Venetian?' she asked.

'Yes, but not an antique. I had it made for the flat. The wood is cherry and the swans were inspired by the finials on Gabriele d'Annunzio's bed in the Casetta delle Rose. My swans are slightly more streamlined.' He put his hand on the one nearest to him. 'No one else has ever slept here apart from myself. I had the bed made as a marriage bed. Perhaps I had a premonition that it wouldn't be long before I met you.'

It was a romantic thing to say, and he looked romantic as he said it, his hair ruffled by the breeze blowing across the lagoon, his tall frame now coatless, an open-necked shirt under a coral sweater making him look younger than the formal suit he had worn earlier in the day.

She had an almost overpowering longing to fling herself into his arms and tell him she loved him. But she mastered it, saying only, 'It's a beautiful bed. I'm honoured to be the first woman to sleep in it.'

He beckoned her to him. 'Do you realise we haven't even kissed each other properly yet? That peck in the register office hardly counts.'

'I know.' His hand was still on the swan when she stepped close to him and put her arms round him.

She couldn't say what she felt, but she could show it, and would, in every way possible. Now that she was his wife, she needn't hold back from physical displays of love even if the words she wanted to speak would be an embarrassment to him until he started to feel the same way about her.

From now on she was determined not to think of *if* but *when*...

Looking up at him, she said, 'You know that saying—Life isn't a dress rehearsal? Well, this morning, when I was dressing, I felt that until today my life *has* been a dress rehearsal...and tonight is the opening night of a show which is going to run for the rest of my life.'

Pierce put his arms round her. 'If you go on saying things like that to me and looking so lovely...' His arms tightened, crushing her to him.

CHAPTER TEN

'WHAT are you writing now?' Pierce asked.

They were sitting in the sun in a *caffè* in one of the city's many squares, the only foreigners there, because although people came to Venice for Christmas and New Year they did not come in their thousands as they did for the famous carnival and during the hot summer months.

At this time of year, Venice belonged to the Venetians and to the connoisseurs who knew the city intimately, not the hordes of tourists who stayed for a day or a few hours, often spending more time peering through their viewfinders than imprinting La Serenissima's beauty on their minds' eyes.

Holly had been writing a couple of postcards, but now was scribbling in a notebook, using a pencil and doing a lot of erasing with the rubber on the end of it.

'I'm trying to write a poem,' she said. 'But please don't ask to see it. I haven't got it right. I may never get it right.'

'Do you often write poetry?'

'I don't often have time...or the inspiration.'

'What's inspiring you now?'

'I've called it ''Venetian Days...Venetian Nights''.' She gave him a saucy grin. 'It's a rather erotic poem.'

In matters relating to sex, she could talk to him freely now. Her last shred of shyness had evaporated. You couldn't be shy with a man whose finely sculpted body you knew as well as your own. The only taboo, the only unmentionable word—at least in any personal context—was love.

'In that case I'd better keep quiet and let you commune with your muse.' Pierce returned his attention to the book, bought an hour earlier at the Libreria Internazionale, which he had been dipping into while they drank coffee.

But a smile lingered round his mouth for a moment or two before he became reabsorbed in the text. She knew she had pleased him with her tacit acknowledgement that Venetian nights in the swan bed had given her life a new dimension.

Occupying one of their table's four chairs was yet another of the many large, stylish carriers they had taken back to the flat since their arrival.

On their first full day in Venice, they hadn't got up until lunchtime. In the afternoon he had taken her to the Missoni shop, buying her a long knitted coat combining a dozen colours in a pattern so vivid yet so subtle that it glowed like a priceless rug and felt as warm as her tweed coat but as light and cosy as a sweater.

Every day since then he had insisted on buying her other lovely things. Perhaps because he couldn't yet give her his heart, he seemed to feel a strong need to lavish her with all the material delights Venice had to offer.

But although everything he had bought her was of the finest quality and would last many years—she expected still to be wearing the Missoni coat when she was middle-aged—it was the hours in his arms which had been his best, most memorable gift to her.

He had taken her gently, impatiently, fiercely, swiftly, leisurely—in all the ways a man could make love to a woman.

More than that, he had shown her how to make love to him, which she had known in theory but never put into practice. When she did, it astonished her to find how much pleasure it gave her. Perhaps that was partly because his body, when he was naked, was even more splendid than she had guessed it would be—lithe, lean and still lightly tanned from a September holiday walking in the Picos de Europa.

His clean, smooth skin was as delicious to taste as it was to touch with her fingers. Sometimes, when she was revelling in the freedom to caress him in ways which would have seemed unbelievable only a few weeks ago, he would suddenly give a low groan and his shoulders would come off the bed as he pushed her onto her back and did the same things to her, driving them both wild.

Remembering those moments made her long to repeat them. 'Pierce...can we go home now?' she asked.

'Of course. Is anything the matter?'

'Nothing that half an hour in bed won't put right.'

He lifted a quizzical eyebrow, then signalled for the bill.

When, arm in arm, with him carrying the shopping, they were walking back to the apartment, he said, 'I've been propositioned before, but I've always suspected the motive.'

'How do you mean?'

'I've felt the suggestion was made to please me, rather than because the propositioner really wanted to go to bed with me. I'm beginning to believe that you do.'

'Of course I do,' she said fervently. 'I think I've missed my vocation...that I was born to make love. But only with you, Signor Sutherland.'

'But not only in Venice, I hope.'

Holly looked up at him. 'It will always be special in Venice because this is where it began and the mirrors and the swans make it seem like a wonderful dream from which I'm afraid to wake up.'

'You aren't going to wake up. It will be the same wherever we are. If you want to have mirrors and swans at Talavera, it can be arranged.'

They had come to the entrance to a long covered alley, one of many such passageways in the city. This one was too narrow for them to walk comfortably abreast. Before going ahead of him, Holly stopped and said, 'Perhaps we could have a different kind of swan bed for Talavera, made in the Regency style...you know, *faux* bamboo and painted swans. But the bed isn't really important. It's the person in it who matters. I'd be happy in any old bed as long as you were there with me.'

She knew that her heart was in her eyes as she said it and turned quickly away to hide a message which, if he read it, she hoped he would intercept as corporal rather than emotional.

It seemed that he did. A little way along the passage, she felt his hand on her shoulder, forcing her to a standstill. Turning her round, he pushed her against the wall and held her there with his body. Then he kissed her hard and hungrily on the mouth.

To two Venetian housewives, the sound of whose heels tapping on the flagstones brought the embrace to an end, they might have looked, seen in silhouette from the far end of the passage, like a pair of illicit lovers snatching a few moments' privacy to give vent to frustrated passion.

As Pierce let her go, Holly realised that, but for the interruption, in a few more moments she would have reached the high pitch of ecstasy that belonged somewhere secluded, not in this public place.

Profoundly shaken, she forced her trembling legs to carry her forward, averting her face and keeping close to the wall as she passed the two women coming the other way, one behind the other.

When they emerged into sunlight, by the side of a narrow canal with a stepped bridge crossing it further along, she said, 'You are a devil, Pierce. Do you know what you almost did to me?'

'No more than I did to myself. You could drive a man insane.' He seized her hand and began to walk very fast, his long stride forcing her to run to keep up with him.

'Stop...stop...you'll give me a stitch,' she protested, with a breathless laugh.

He did stop. A moment later, she was in his arms, being carried.

'Pierce...you can't. What will people think?'

'Who cares what they think? If I want to carry you, I will.' He lowered his voice to add softly, 'I will do whatever I want with you, but it will take more than half an hour. It could take all afternoon.'

On their last evening in Venice, they dined at a restaurant which stayed open later than most in a city whose citizens kept early hours, especially in winter.

Afterwards they strolled home through almost deserted streets and over bridges reflected in motionless water. It was almost full moon, although not much moonlight penetrated the narrower streets and canals, where the buildings cast such black shadows that, even though Venice was a safe city at night, in places it had a sinister atmosphere for anyone imaginative.

Then they came out into the great open space of the Piazza San Marco and for once there was no one about. Even the pigeons had gone to their roosts on the ledges and friezes of the surrounding buildings.

'Let's have a last cup of chocolate at Florian's,' Pierce suggested.

'They'll have closed...hours ago,' said Holly regretfully.

Of all the pleasures of Venice, she had particularly liked the city's oldest *caffè* with its many little rooms inside and, outside, musicians playing on an awning-covered dais, their music sometimes mingling with that of the rival *caffè* the Quadri, on the opposite side of the square.

But at this hour, both would shut and, by the time they reopened, she and her husband would be on their way to the airport. The honeymoon would be over.

'Do you know any old-fashioned dances?' Pierce asked as they were crossing the Piazza. 'The waltz and the tango, for instance?'

'Strangely enough, I do. My father showed me how to waltz and I learnt a bit of the tango—not the very complicated steps—for a show we put on at college. Do you know any ballroom dances?'

'I've been to a few formal balls. I can put on a reasonable show. Would you like to try me?' He turned and assumed the posture of a dancing partner.

As they had the square to themselves, Holly didn't hang back. She thought they would take a few turns and then he would kiss her and hustle her home for their last night in the swan bed.

'They say that one of the cafés is haunted,' he said as she put her hand on his shoulder. 'People living around the square or walking home in the small hours have sometimes heard music playing. But when they look out from their windows or come round the corner it suddenly stops.'

'It sounds like something cooked up by the tourist office,' said Holly, knowing he wouldn't believe in such a story.

He drew her closer, beginning to whistle one of the slow sweet numbers from the *caffè* musicians' repertoire. As he put his cheek against her temple, Holly closed her eyes, the better to concentrate on what her feet should be doing.

Then, as they slowly revolved and he shifted his hold on her hand to interlace their fingers, she heard a violin starting to pick up the melody, and then a cello and a piano.

Her eyes flew open. She looked round. The arcade in front of Florian's was now alight and on the dais, also lit up, three musicians in overcoats and fur hats were smiling and nodding to her.

'Did you plan this? Is it just for us?'

Pierce was grinning from ear to ear like a delighted schoolboy who had pulled off a great practical joke.

'Just for you, my lovely. Something special to remember when we're back in the everyday world.'

'Oh, Pierce, it's *all* been special…every single minute. You told me I'd fall for Venice and I have…head over heels.'

And for you, too, my darling love.

She almost blurted it out but just managed not to.

They danced to a half-hour medley of waltzes and tangos, Holly's confidence growing as she found that their physical harmony also extended to dancing. Anything he did, she could follow. In the end they were whirling and twirling like a couple of professionals.

When the music finally stopped and she rested, breathless, in his arms, the musicians applauded. One of them had brought a large flask of hot chocolate and some of the pastries sold in the *caffè* by day, and a bottle of *grappa*, a spirit that seared Holly's throat but made her attempt more polite remarks in Italian than she might otherwise have done. Pierce, of course, spoke it fluently and was able to thank them more graciously than she could, before they all said goodnight.

'I'll remember it all my life,' she told him, on the way home. 'I'll tell our grandchildren about it. "When we were on our honeymoon, your grandfather hired an orchestra to dance with me in the Piazza.'' I wonder if anyone else has ever done that? I shouldn't imagine so. Most men would never think of it.'

Whereupon, to her dismay, she burst into tears and had to pretend she was crying from happiness.

But the real reason was that she found it unbearably painful to have everything in the world any woman could possibly want, except the freedom to say those three little words, 'I love you'.

In the time between their return to London and his departure with Ben for Argentina, Pierce was away a great deal. His absences allowed Holly to get on with her work in Norfolk, taking Parson with her for company. But, fond as she was of her cat, he was an unsatisfactory proxy for her husband.

In late January, Pierce managed to make time to take her to spend a long weekend with his parents. She hoped they liked her. She liked them even more than she had expected to.

Soon after this came the day when they had to say goodbye for five weeks. To Holly it seemed an eternity of loneliness and anxiety. Although the mountain the men were tackling wasn't comparable with the great peaks of the Himalaya, it was sufficiently hazardous for more than a hundred people to have died attempting to reach the summit.

While he was gone she went down to Talavera and began a comprehensive survey of the grounds. It wasn't a job which could be completed quickly, but she hoped to have it ready to show Pierce when he came home...if he came home.

From Mendoza, the city in western Argentina where those attempting the climb had their last taste of civilisa-

tion, he called her. She managed to sound bright and cheerful. It wasn't the way she was feeling.

As soon as he had rung off, she wished she had told him
she loved him. What did it matter that he didn't feel the
same way? At least, if something should happen to him,
she would have told him the truth, held nothing back. Not
knowing where they were staying, she couldn't ring him.
The opportunity was lost and might never recur.

The feeling that she had been wrong to conceal her feelings oppressed her more as the time passed. It passed interminably slowly. Every night she watched the newscast
with mounting dread that one of the last, minor items in
the catalogue of death and disaster would be a fatal accident
on Aconcagua. Every morning she switched on the radio
feeling the same apprehension.

Hooper, who sensed her anxiety, although she tried to
hide it, would boost her morale by citing examples of his
employer's ability to get himself out of trouble, including
several sticky situations in central African conflicts.

Every week she had a call from her mother-in-law whom
she knew was equally anxious although, like Holly, she
didn't admit to it.

One day, while they were talking, Marianne Sutherland
said, 'It was such a relief to me when Pierce fell in love
with you. I was beginning to wonder if he would ever find
someone to suit him…if he had passed the stage when he
was capable of falling in love. And then he called us to say
he had met this amazing girl who was everything he'd ever
dreamed of…but that she didn't like him.'

This was followed by hoots of maternal laughter at the
idea of anyone being able to resist one of her beloved sons.

Holly managed to laugh too. 'Did he really say that about
me…even before I changed my mind about him?'

'Oh, yes, he was plainly besotted. In fact we were a bit

worried. For someone like Pierce to fall headlong in love at first sight seemed out of character. We wondered if it could last. But once we had met you we understood.'

'I wish I did,' Holly answered. 'I know why I love your son, but why he should love me is baffling.'

And even more baffling is why he should tell *you* he loves me, but never tell *me* he loves me, she was thinking.

'I don't think people ever recognise why they themselves are lovable,' said her mother-in-law. 'The lucky ones, like you and me, who are loved by very special men just have to accept that it is so and be eternally grateful.'

After that conversation, Holly debated flying out to Mendoza to be there when Pierce got back. It was Hooper who dissuaded her, pointing out that if there had been any change of plan she might find it hard to locate him, especially as she didn't speak Spanish.

On the day before they were due back, Chiara rang up. Immersed in her own concerns, Holly had hardly given a thought to what might be happening to her stepsister. Now she learned that Eric had been dropped and Chiara was living on the yacht of the man who had given her the aquamarine. She sounded on top of the world.

'He's gorgeous…and he's crazy about me…wants me to meet his family. They're in Australia. His father's a motor-cruiser tycoon and his mother comes from Indonesia, which explains why, when I saw him, I thought Bradley might be a sheikh.'

'Are you going to Australia on his yacht?' Holly asked, a good deal relieved that Chiara's new man was Australian and not from a culture where attitudes to women were completely different from those in the West.

'No, that would take too long,' said Chiara. 'Bradley and I will fly there. The yacht can be shipped back the same way it came to Europe. So it doesn't look as if you and I'll be seeing much of each other in future, Hol. Bradley's had Europe, he says. He wanted to have a look round but he likes his own country better. He says the future is with the Pacific Rim countries. He says...'

She talked about Bradley non-stop for the next ten minutes. If he was only half as opinionated as she made him sound, he must be a world-class bore, thought Holly. All the same she was glad Chiara had met the man she had always wanted: rich, generous, handsome, pleasure-loving and besotted with her.

Perhaps down under she could make a fresh start, as so many others had. If the relationship lasted, Australia could be the making of her.

'So it's goodbye for now, but I'll give you a buzz every now and then,' Chiara promised.

'Yes, do that. Don't let's lose touch. Take care of yourself.'

As she replaced the receiver, Holly had the feeling it could be goodbye for a long time, if not for ever.

It was five o'clock in the morning when Pierce rang from Mendoza to say they had made the summit and would soon be flying to Buenos Aires and then back to London.

'Have you been OK, Holly? I've been worried about you.'

'I've been fine, but missing you badly. I can't wait for you to come home. Saying "I love you" on the telephone isn't the same as saying it in person.'

When he didn't answer, she had a sinking feeling that they had been cut off in mid-call.

Then his voice came through, strong and clear. 'Say it again anyway.'

'I love you. I've always loved you. Perhaps from the first time we met, when you belonged to someone else.'

'I never belonged to anyone till that day at New Covent Garden when you made it clear me you hated my guts. From that day on I was hooked.'

'Do you realise you've never said so?'

'Neither have you, until now.'

'I know…it's been driving me crazy…that something awful might happen and I would never have told you in so many words.'

'It's been the same for me, I pictured you getting run over…being in a train smash. Why the hell am I up here, stuck in this damned tent with Ben, when I could be in bed with Holly? I kept asking myself.'

'Pierce, have you called your parents? They've been as anxious as I was.'

'I know and I'll do that next. But you had priority. You're more important than anyone. I'll be with you as soon as I can. Until then, take care of yourself.'

Why it had been a problem to be open about their feelings was something that they discussed some hours after their reunion. By then they had made rapturous love and Pierce had caught up on some sleep.

The exertion of the ascent combined with limited food had made him lose weight. He was all bone and sinew—too spare, in her opinion, but even more exciting with his lean face deeply tanned by the Argentine sun and his hair overdue for a cut.

'Until I was stuck on that mountain, unable to make contact with you, I'd never been in a situation where, if something went wrong, I would leave a dependant…someone I wanted to be with for the rest of my life,' Pierce said thoughtfully. 'Before that I was hell-bent on inducing you to love me, which I didn't think you did.'

'Why did you think I married you?'

'Partly for Talavera. Partly because of the sexual attraction between us. Partly because you were lonely. Put together, those factors seemed enough for you to persuade yourself that marrying me was a sensible thing to do.'

'It *was* a sensible thing to do,' Holly said, smiling. 'Men like you aren't thick on the ground. Any woman who meets one is a fool if she hesitates…even if there is a downside.'

'What's the downside?' Pierce asked, amused.

They were having a late breakfast in the conservatory, with Parson and Louisa sunning themselves on the long, cushioned window-seat and a vase of early daffodils flown in from the Scilly Islands on the table.

'The downside is having to bite one's nails when you're risking your neck on the other side of the world. But if all our reunions are going to be like this one I guess it's a small price to pay.'

'It wasn't much of a risk and I may give up doing these things now that my home life has become more exciting,' he said, reaching for her hand and pressing it to his cheek. 'I love you in ways there are no words to explain.'

He hadn't shaved yet and she felt a tingle of response to the masculine roughness of his bristles against her palm. She knew that being married wouldn't change him and she didn't want him to change. His energy and his daring were two of the many reasons why she loved him.

Why such a man should love her must remain forever a mystery.

Let's Celebrate!

LOVE & LAUGHTER™

invites you to
the party of the season!

Grab your popcorn and be prepared to laugh as we celebrate with **LOVE & LAUGHTER**.

Harlequin's newest series is going Hollywood!

Let us make you laugh with three months of terrific books, authors and romance, plus a chance to win a FREE 15-copy video collection of the best romantic comedies ever made.

For more details look in the back pages of any Love & Laughter title, from July to September, at your favorite retail outlet.

Don't forget the popcorn!

Available wherever
Harlequin books are sold.

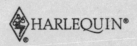
♦ HARLEQUIN®

Look us up on-line at: http://www.romance.net

LLCELEB

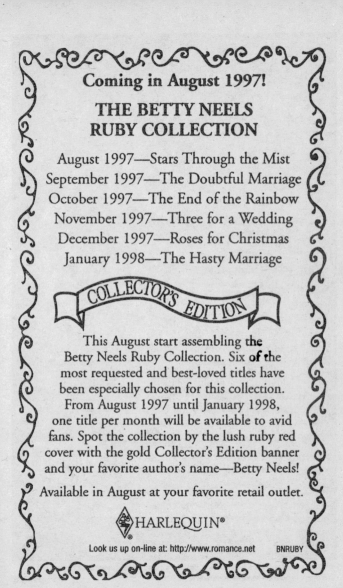

Coming in August 1997!

THE BETTY NEELS RUBY COLLECTION

August 1997—Stars Through the Mist
September 1997—The Doubtful Marriage
October 1997—The End of the Rainbow
November 1997—Three for a Wedding
December 1997—Roses for Christmas
January 1998—The Hasty Marriage

COLLECTOR'S EDITION

This August start assembling the
Betty Neels Ruby Collection. Six of the
most requested and best-loved titles have
been especially chosen for this collection.
From August 1997 until January 1998,
one title per month will be available to avid
fans. Spot the collection by the lush ruby red
cover with the gold Collector's Edition banner
and your favorite author's name—Betty Neels!

Available in August at your favorite retail outlet.

HARLEQUIN®

HARLEQUIN WOMEN KNOW ROMANCE WHEN THEY SEE IT.

And they'll see it on **ROMANCE CLASSICS**, the new 24-hour TV channel devoted to romantic movies and original programs like the special **Harlequin® Showcase of Authors & Stories.**

The **Harlequin® Showcase of Authors & Stories** introduces you to many of your favorite romance authors in a program developed exclusively for Harlequin® readers.

Watch for the **Harlequin® Showcase of Authors & Stories** series beginning in the summer of 1997.

ROMANCE CLASSICS™

If you're not receiving ROMANCE CLASSICS, call your local cable operator or satellite provider and ask for it today!

Escape to the network of your dreams.